THE Happiness QUEST

Rebekkah Edlund

ISBN 979-8-9891564-0-5

Cover Art by: Roy Edlund

Cover Photo by: Dane Dupuis

Library of Congress Control Number: 2023921333

Printed in the United States of America

For my parents

Never stop dreaming and true love never dies.

*My mother's love has been the thing that makes
the universe go round, and my father has been
the sun in the center of it.*

I love you.

TABLE OF CONTENTS

CHAPTER 1

What had my life been like before? Normal. That's what it had been. Monotonous, mundane, and boring.

I mean, I guess it had been fine, really. Nothing was necessarily wrong. My life was better than a lot of people's, if I had taken the time to think about it. I lived in the sunshine state and had a good job as a hair stylist at a boutique salon. I had a few close friends, and a lot of acquaintances. My mom was the only family I had, but she was pretty much my best friend, so the lack of other family never seemed to matter. There was no boyfriend in the picture, but I dated occasionally and held out hope that one day my best friend Pete and I would get together. Even with all that, I was just uninspired and bored.

Everything started to change, though, the day I was bemoaning my lack-luster life to my mom. I had spent the night at her house, and was now sitting at her kitchen table, staring into my coffee. The soft music coming from the other room was the only sound.

I looked up from my coffee, my mom was sitting across from me, waiting patiently for me to speak.

"I just feel like all the movies promise us a happily ever after. This doesn't feel like I'm even on the road to happily-ever-after. I'm stuck in the same cycles. Go to work, to pay the bills. Go out with friends so you forget that you hate your life, and rinse and repeat day after day. I'm 34, isn't life supposed to be more than this by now?" My frustrations were just pouring out, and I continued, "I mean, maybe, some years I can afford to go on a trip with my friends, but mostly I am just working my life away. Is this what life is supposed to be, Mom? Is this all there is?"

My mom had let me rant with her usual quiet smile. She wasn't super emotional, and she didn't always understand me, but she always listened. I knew I was lucky because I had never doubted that she loved me with every fiber of her being.

I took a sip from my mug, "Black and bitter like my soul."

"Oh, Willa," my mom replied finally. "Your soul isn't black or bitter, if it was, you wouldn't be aching for more. We just need to figure out what makes you feel alive."

"I know. But, it's just why don't more people break out into song and dance like they do in all the Disney movies? That's the kind of happy that I want. I don't need a musical, I just want to be happy. There's something missing, Mom, and I don't know what it is."

"Do you think it's the fact that you're not in love, and you're wishing for a relationship?" my mom asked. She was not one to beat around the bush.

I met her eyes, startled. "No! I don't need a Prince Charming. Although, I wouldn't complain if one came around. But you might be right when you say that about being in love. Whenever I've been in love, the world seems magical, everything is good, and if it's not, I can see past the issues," I paused for a moment to conclude my thoughts. "That is the happiness feeling that I'm looking for, but I don't want to have it because I'm in love with some guy. I want to have it because I'm in love with life, but I'm just not. It's so boring."

My mom didn't answer right away, letting me stew in my thoughts. But then she laughed suddenly, startling me and I looked up at her, the wordless question written on my face.

"I was just thinking that you should go to the woods and have an adventure. But then I realized that the Lord of the Rings soundtrack is playing right now, and that might be why I thought of that." She was still chuckling.

I grinned back at her.

"I just think you need to get lost in nature and see if you can do some soul searching," she said seriously. "Everyone's version of happiness is a little bit different, but I think if you go to the woods, and immerse yourself in nature, you'll be able to pinpoint what your version is."

"But why the woods?" I asked, puzzled.

"Because it's quiet, because life is simpler away from the city. It's easy to get lost here in the chaos of the city. Nature slows everything down and gives you space and the freedom to think and breathe. One of the happiest times of my life was when your father and I spent time in the smoky mountains before you were born."

I never got tired of hearing about my dad. He had died before I turned four and I barely remembered him. My mom had never remarried. She had told me one time that he had been her true love, and she didn't want to find someone else to fill the gap his death had caused.

"What happened that made it the happiest?"

"Nothing happened. Maybe that's why it was so good. We rented a cabin, went on hikes, and cooked food over the fire. Your dad had brought his guitar and wrote a song for me. We were just so in love and laughed so much."

"That sounds lovely." My mind went to Peter. He and I always laughed a lot too.

"Are you thinking about Peter?"

I felt my face flush with embarrassment. "I don't like you reading my mind, Mom."

She shook her head. "I just wish that you weren't so hung up on him. If it was meant to be, you two would be together by now. I think he takes you for granted, and I hate that."

I sighed, "I know you don't like him, but we have so much fun together." My tone was wistful.

"No, baby, it's not that I don't like him. He's charming and witty. I can see why you're attracted to him. But you have been friends for two years, and he's dated a myriad of women in that time, but never you. I would like to see you with someone who thinks you are the reason the moon shines at night and believes that you are made of magic. I don't want you to settle for less than that. Because, when you find someone who thinks that of you, and you think the same of him, that is true love, and it can weather all the storms of life."

Tears had sprung to my eyes while she spoke. "But, Mom, I feel like I'm getting so old. Everyone is in a relationship or are divorced from their first and heading for their second. What if I'm destined to be single forever? That's why this is my desperate attempt to figure out happiness. I need to be happy with that destiny, I need to be happy without a guy. If one happens along, great, but if not? I still want my happily ever after."

My mom got up and put her hand on my shoulder, squeezing reassuringly. "You're going to find it, baby. I promise. I still think that you should run away to the mountains and the trees for a bit. Go on a quest."

I laughed outright, there were rare moments when my mom would say shockingly weird things. "A quest?"

"Yep," she grinned down at me. "I was just keeping with the theme of the music."

"Alright," I conceded, smiling back up at her, "a happiness quest it is."

She gave my shoulder another squeeze and went over to the refrigerator. "Ready for breakfast?"

"Yes," a thought struck me, "Mom, if I'm going on a quest, does that mean that I can have second breakfast too?"

"Absolutely, but let's figure out the first right now."

We both laughed. The despair that had been gripping my heart eased as we made breakfast together.

I left my mom's house a few hours later feeling better, and excited to start planning a trip. The only damper was that it was the beginning of May, and my salon chair was always full at this time of year. Graduations were in full swing, along with Mother's Day and prepping for the summer break. It seemed like everyone needed a touch up on their hair. This was money season, and I wasn't sure that I should take time off right now. But I'd promised my mom that I'd look into it before I left her, and I would.

My phone rang soon after getting in my car and my heart skipped a beat. It was Peter. He didn't usually call me during the workday. I always had a day off during the week since I worked most Saturdays, but he was in environmental law, and would be at work right now.

"Hey! Everything okay?" I asked immediately, answering the phone.

"Yeah, of course. How are you?"

"I'm alright," I responded, "what's up?"

"Just checking on you," he said.

I smiled, "That's nice. Thanks for that. It seems like we've been busy this month and haven't talked as much as usual."

"Yeah," he hesitated, "About that, I need to talk to you about something that I've been putting off for a little while."

"This doesn't sound good. Should I be worried right now?"

"Just let me get this out," he pleaded, "I've been seeing someone for the past month."

"Ohhh!" I took a deep breath. That was unexpected. He had never minded telling me about who he was dating before now.

I braced myself as he continued, "I didn't tell you because I wasn't sure if it was going to get serious or not. But it is getting serious. I think I'm in love."

"Wow." My head was spinning now, but it wasn't fair to tell him that. "Pete, you know I want you to be happy."

"I know," he replied, "but there's always been this unspoken thing between us, like we might go there if we ever gave it a chance."

"Yeah." I hesitated a moment, what could I do besides just play it off? He was my best friend, and I did truly want him to be happy. But... why did he have to go and find someone else when I was right here?

"I do care about you, Pete. You being in an actual relationship will change everything, so that is going to suck for me. But your happiness is more important."

"I'm so sorry, Willa. You're important too. I don't want this to change things or affect our friendship, because you know I care about you also."

"Peter," I said, my tone was firm, I felt like I was using the same tone as my mom did when she was trying to drive a point home, "as much as neither of us want it to change things, it will. You know it too." I felt like I was cutting out my heart with each word. I knew that there would be no more late night phone calls. No more telling each other everything. She'd become his best friend and more, and I would take a back seat. I swallowed the lump in my throat as I continued, "I'm glad you told me, though. She does make you happy, right?"

"Yeah, she really does." His voice got softer, "She just feels like home."

There was a sudden sharp pain in my heart, but I smiled as I replied so that he wouldn't know, "I'm so happy for you! Let's get lunch tomorrow and you can tell me all about her."

My feelings were a mess when we got off the phone. I wanted to be sincerely happy, because of course I wanted that for him. But why had he never tried with me? Was he just not attracted to me like that? I thought of the times that we had come close to kissing, but something had always interrupted the moment. We had briefly talked about it at one point, and he had said that he didn't want to mess up our friendship. I guess I had just assumed that eventually things would fall into place, because aren't all the best relationships based on friendships? A tear escaped and ran down my cheek. I brushed it away, willing myself not to cry. I needed to wait until I wasn't driving.

Everything would change now, even if he thought that it wouldn't. I thought about how we were used to talking pretty much every day after work and at least a few texts throughout the day and swallowed hard. I would miss those late night conversations that were soul-baring in their intensity. We would meet up at least once a week for lunch or drinks, or a game night at our favorite hangout spot. I realized with that thought that he'd probably want to bring her along now. The pit in my stomach was not getting better.

I pulled into my parking spot and went quickly up the stairs to my condo. I needed to let it all out and cry so that tomorrow when I met him for lunch, I would be able to put on a brave face and be happy for him. Today, though, I was going to be sad for myself.

CHAPTER 2

I woke up the next morning feeling better. The tears I had shed yesterday over my dashed hopes had relieved some of the tension, and sleep had helped even more.

I rolled out of bed and got dressed. Gina would be opening with me at the salon, so I would be able to get some solid friend time in before meeting Peter for lunch. I had texted her the headlines last night, but hadn't been ready to talk about it in detail.   Today she'd want to know the whole story, and I would tell her everything.

I eyed myself in the mirror and touched the bags under my eyes. That's what I get for crying over a boy. I applied the little makeup that I wore and headed out the door. Hopefully they would disappear by lunchtime. I didn't want Peter to know. He might find out because he was friends with Gina too, but hopefully she wouldn't share too much. He probably wouldn't even ask her anything if he was as smitten with this new girl as he seemed to be.

Bitterness was still trying to win out against my better self which was happy for him. I shoved those feelings as far down as I could and turned up my music to drown all thoughts away as I drove to work.

Gina was waiting for me in the parking lot since I was the one with the keys to the salon. She and I had been best friends since we were in cosmetology school together ten years ago.

She was laughing as I turned down the radio and rolled up my windows.

"Are you trying to convert the neighborhood to Tom Petty?" she called over to me.

"Would that be the worst thing ever?" I replied, with a wink. "No, I just needed to avoid my thoughts and singing loudly with Tom Petty seemed like my best option."

Gina swallowed her laughter. "I'm really sorry about Pete, babe."

"Yeah," I replied. "Me too. I just always thought…"

"I did too. I mean, I was starting to get annoyed that after all this time you two weren't official, because it's been obvious to anyone with eyes that you guys are perfect together."

"Not to him, I guess," I said, unlocking the door and holding it open for her. "Gina, he said she feels like home." The despair of yesterday still seeping out in my tone.

"Oh, honey," she was sympathetic.

"In other news," I said, choosing to get out of this depressing topic as I set up my station, "I was talking to my mom yesterday at breakfast, and she suggested that I go on a quest."

"What?" Gina stopped what she was doing and stared at me.

I laughed.

"I was ranting to her about how boring and unfulfilling life feels to me right now. She thinks that I'll be able to figure things out if I just go to the woods for a while."

"Oh my God! This is incredible. So, it's going to be a quest? Are you going for Lord of the Rings vibes or Disney Princess? Please say Disney Princess." Gina's face was alight with laughter. This was my favorite thing about her. She laughed so easily.

"Yes! That's what I said! I want to be singing and dancing with the forest creatures."

"Yes! Can I come too?"

"No." I grinned at her.

She wasn't offended, as I knew she wouldn't be.

"Will you at least wear a princess dress when you go and take a video for me?"

"Oh, you're the worst." We were both laughing now. "Maybe," I conceded.

"Yes! Willa, you have to do this."

Our first appointments of the day walked in, and the conversations shifted. I still felt like a ball of emotion that was just trying to ignore everything. I couldn't seem to get away from feeling like I was losing my best friend to some girl who "felt like home." *How could he say that when I was the one who had been there with him through thick and thin for the past two years? I was his emergency contact since his family lived out of state. But she was home?* I knew that I was overreacting and felt stupid because of it. On the flip side, I was also excited to plan a trip to the woods, but also scared, because I had no idea what I was going to do, or how it would even help. There was just no fire in my veins, no pizzaz. *And, god damn Peter.*

I shook my head, trying to get out of my thoughts.

"Are you alright, dear?" Mrs. McCarthy asked, looking at me in the mirror, watching as I painted her roots.

"Oh, yes, love," I replied, "I'm sorry, I was just thinking about something else. How is Princess Effy doing? I swear you have the most regal cat I've ever seen."

Mrs. McCarthy smiled, her face lighting up. Her cat was one thing she never grew tired of talking about.

The morning seemed to fly by after that, the usual rhythms of work helped get my mind back on track. Lunch with Peter was looming, though, and I knew that it wasn't going to be my favorite time we'd ever spent together.

I texted him as I left the salon, the little Mexican restaurant we'd meet at was just two doors down from me, and a short drive for him from his work.

"Just walked out the door," I sent. "See you in a bit!"

The little dots appeared as he started replying immediately.

"Here. Got us a table."

I sent a thumbs up and quickened my walk.

I saw him immediately when I walked in the restaurant, he was seated in a booth off to the right. He looked over at me and smiled, my heart skipped a beat. He wasn't the tallest man ever, but he was well proportioned. His bright blue eyes always seemed to see into my soul and his smile took my breath away. He stood up to give me a hug as I approached the table.

"Hey!"

"Hey!" I smiled back at him. I was glad he had still hugged me when he saw me. At least that was still the same.

We sat down.

"So, I actually have stuff to tell you too, by the way." I said, not wanting things to get awkward right away.

"Oh, yeah?"

"Yeah, it's pretty crazy," I grinned at him.

The server came over just at that moment, and we ordered our regular choices. I always got the chicken quesadilla with beans and rice, and Peter always got the mojo burrito. Most of the servers knew our order, but this was a new one that I'd only seen maybe twice before. When he left the table, I turned back to look at Peter. He was smiling at me again, and his eyes seemed to twinkle.

"Alright, tell me this crazy story. Although, this is you, I mean, when are your stories ever not crazy?"

"Very true," I conceded, I usually kept him entertained with stories of my clients. "Okay, so I spent the night at my mom's the other day, like I told you. But what I didn't tell you, is that the next morning I had a long talk with her."

"Oh my god," he interrupted me, dramatically. "You talked to your mom? That IS crazy."

"Stop, asshole," I laughed, "That's not the crazy part."

He was grinning at me with a mischievous twinkle in his eyes. I made myself ignore how good it felt to laugh with him, and I continued, "My mom thinks I should go on a quest in the woods and Gina thinks that I should make it a Disney Princess quest."

He laughed, as I knew he would, but then frowned slightly in confusion, "Okay, but why? I mean, I know why Gina said that, she's a Disney freak. But what's the purpose of a quest? And why is it a quest?"

"Well, so, my mom and I were talking about how I've just been feeling blah about everything, and I told her that I want my life to feel like it has a happily ever after."

His face blanched. I could tell that my words hit him hard, and that he had taken it the wrong way.

"Oh, Peter, that's not what I meant!" I exclaimed hastily. "I just want to be happy, and I don't want it to have anything to do with the people in my life or the circumstances that I find myself in. I just want to figure out how to live happily."

"Okay," he replied, still hesitant. "But I still don't understand what that has to do with the woods and a quest?"

"The quest part was because the Lord of the Rings soundtrack was playing, and we thought it was funny. My mom said that life is simpler in the woods, and basically the idea is, that by going and escaping the chaos of the city, I might find that happiness inside of myself. She said that her and my dad had the happiest time of their lives there."

He didn't say anything for a few moments, just sat there staring at his drink as if suddenly it was the strangest thing he'd ever seen. I waited, but then he looked up at me again and smiled briefly.

"I think that's wonderful. You should definitely do this."

"I know. It's so crazy though, right?" I replied, relieved. "I truly have no idea what I'm doing or even where I'm going to go yet," I continued after a pause. "I have no idea if I'll figure out anything, or experience anything more than tramping through the woods. But I really feel like I owe it to myself to get out of this blasé feeling. I'm alive, shouldn't even that make me happy?"

One of the workers brought our food, interrupting my train of thought.

"Thank you." We smiled at the food runner appreciatively.

"Do you need anything else?" she asked.

Peter and I looked at each other and shook our heads. "Nope."

"Enjoy then," she replied as she turned away.

The food looked amazing, and we dove in. After a few bites Peter looked over at me. "This quest of yours sounds like it's going to be pretty incredible. I should probably do something like that too sometime. Are you going to go soon?"

For a reason I couldn't place, a knot gripped my stomach. *Was it fear? What was I scared of?* "I don't know, honestly, I haven't really had much time to think about it."

"Well, I can't wait to hear what happens for you."

"Yeah, I really think it's going to be epic," I replied. "When I was telling Gina about it this morning, she came up with the Disney Princess vibe and wants me to at least film myself singing and dancing in the woods."

Peter cracked up laughing, "Oh my god, I love Gina. Are you going to do it?"

"I can't let her down! I'll have to bring a princess dress with me just for it." I grinned back at him, and continued, "Do you want to talk about your stuff now?"

I killed the mood with those words. I had known I would, but I also felt like I was waiting for my guillotined death, and it was time to just get it out of the way.

He let out a little sigh. "Well, her name is Vanessa. I met her at a work thing the beginning of last month."

My mind raced, trying to remember what work thing that was, he had had a couple different ones. "The chamber party?"

"Oh, you remember?"

"Yeah," I replied. *Didn't he realize that I knew everything about him? I pay attention when he tells me things.* I had just assumed he was busy, but now that I knew, I could definitely see that things had started changing after that.

"So, Vanessa is a corporate attorney. She came to the party with Jim and his girlfriend. It turns out that it was an attempt to set us up, but neither of us knew about it beforehand. Anyway, we just really hit it off that evening, and we've been talking ever since."

"Do you have a picture of her?" I asked, curious to see this person that had stolen Peter's heart away from me. *Not that it was ever mine.* I reminded myself harshly.

"Yeah. We took this picture a couple days ago," he said, smiling at the memory as he swiped open his phone. The background was a picture of them smiling. She was an exquisite dark haired petite woman. *There's no way I even compare,* I thought miserably, thinking of my unruly red curls and freckles. They looked so happy together.

I looked up at him, he was still smiling down at the picture. *Oh my gosh, he really is in love.*

"You two are so cute," I said. "Tell me more about her though, what is she like?"

"Well, I guess what really stole my heart is how much fun she is. We laugh all the time. We've been doing the typical date nights with dinner and drinks, Top Golf, we've even gone bowling."

He paused, thinking, "She's really into sports, and plays basketball and softball. From what I hear, she's one of the top players in her firm's softball league. But she's also intelligent and well read, she likes good music. Oh, and she has a dog, a little spaniel mix that's pretty much the most adorable thing ever."

"Ah! That's what hooked you," I teased him. "You're in love with her dog."

He grinned back at me. "Yes, yes I am."

CHAPTER 3

I excused myself and escaped to the bathroom after I'd finished my plate. I needed a moment to regroup.

I stood in front of the mirror, willing the tears to stay in. I had been mentally comparing myself to Vanessa. My long curly flaming red hair and green eyes were my best features, I thought, but I wasn't as perfect as she looked to be. My face was attractive enough, and the men I dated had always complimented me on my dimples. I was active and mostly in shape, but my figure wasn't perfect, at least in my eyes.

I sighed. Vanessa, though, she did look perfect. She had perfect hair, perfect make-up, tiny hourglass figure, fun and athletic too, of course Peter fell for her.

I took a deep breath and turned away from the mirror, I couldn't stay in here forever. I left the bathroom and returned to the table where Peter was waiting.

"I don't want to ask this, Peter," I said, sliding back into my seat. "But what do you think our friendship will look like now? I don't know if it will be right or fair to her if we continue to talk every day."

He looked stricken. "I don't want to think about that. Why does it have to change?"

I just looked at him, I knew there was pain in my eyes too.

"You could just meet her, and then she'd know there was nothing to be jealous of. She'd see that we're just best friends."

"Is that what she'd see, though?" I asked, gently.

He was quiet again, staring down at the table, fiddling with his napkin. The server had cleared our plates while I was in the bathroom.

I thought about all the phone calls, the texts, the occasional flirty conversations. Yes, I was his best friend, but also something a little bit more.

"I do want to meet her," I said, continuing. "Of course I do if she means this much to you. Although, I might need a little bit of time."

"I'm so sorry. I didn't mean to hurt you." He looked haunted, and I felt so bad for him.

"No, it's okay. Peter, I'm so glad you found someone you're in love with. I want you to be happy more than anything. It's just going to take me a second to get used to the idea of not having your undivided attention." I smiled at him, "It's going to be okay."

"I don't know what to say," he replied. "What do you want to do now? Not talk anymore?"

"That's not what I was trying to say." Now it was my turn to be hurt. "I don't think it has to be all or nothing. I was just trying to say that maybe we need to not be the first person we tell everything to. I don't know. I don't know how to navigate this either. I'm just trying to do what's right... and fair to all of us."

Our server brought our check and interrupted us. We gave him our cards and he turned away to go run them.

Peter and I just stared at the table, occasionally glancing up to see what the other was thinking, and to see if the other one would speak. I hated this tension, and now I was miserable. The server brought our checks back and wished us a wonderful day. I flashed him a brief smile. It wasn't his fault that it wasn't a good day at all.

"Ready?" Peter asked.

I nodded, and we stood up. We walked out the front door and then paused.

"I don't like how we're leaving this," Peter said abruptly.

"I don't either." There were tears in my eyes.

He reached out and pulled me in for a hug. We stood like that for a long minute and then stepped away.

"I don't like the idea of putting limits on us talking. I mean, if something funny or important happens, we'll still text. But maybe just not everything else, and that will break the habit of talking all the time."

I nodded up at him. "Okay." My tone was sad.

"This was your idea," he said, "I don't like it any more than you do. But you were probably right to call us out on it."

I nodded again and tried to smile at him. "So, I guess I'll see you in a few weeks."

He looked stricken. "A few weeks? Why a few weeks?"

"I'm going to need some time." My tone was subdued, the prospect of not seeing him for a while was not my favorite thought either. But I also felt like if I had to meet Vanessa at game night this week or even next week, I'd probably be shitty to her. She didn't deserve that, and neither did he. So, a few weeks was probably for the best.

Peter nodded, "Okay. I really am sorry, you know."

"I know," I said, turning away. But then I turned back and gave him another hug. "It'll be okay," I murmured. "I'm going to try to go on this quest sooner rather than later, and when I get back, I'll have so much to tell you."

"I know you will. I'm excited for you." He smiled at me and waved as he headed back to work.

I walked back to the salon feeling numb. I was going to have to come up with something to occupy my time so that I wouldn't realize how much I was missing him. Planning the trip would help. Getting out of town would probably be the best thing for me right now. I took a deep breath and opened the door. Time to get back to work.

Gina didn't have a client when I walked in. She took one look at my face, and came to wrap her arms around me, "It's going to be okay."

The tears started flowing, I couldn't hold them in any longer. "She's just perfect, Gina."

"So are you!" she exclaimed. "Don't let yourself feel otherwise."

"Well, she's more perfect."

Gina chuckled, still hugging me tightly. "Maybe she snores like a freight train."

I let go of Gina and wiped my eyes, smiling. "Maybe so."

"We decided that we need to get out of the habit of talking every day about everything, and I'm not going to see him for a few weeks," I told her.

"Holy shit! That sounds a bit extreme."

"I know, but neither one of us knows how to handle this, and it's not fair to continue as we were."

"Well, I mean, I guess this is a choice you both have to make." She sighed, and then added, "I think you might be making a mountain out of a mole hill, though. Guys and girls can be friends, and it's not like Peter is marrying this goddess just yet."

"Oh, don't even say that, Gina. I don't want to think about him marrying her!" I exclaimed, "I just want to do what's right. I know it might be a little over the top, but I keep putting myself in her shoes. If roles were reversed, would I feel comfortable knowing that he was this close to some other girl? Besides, I don't want to have to meet her for a little while, not until I can actually be happy for them."

I sighed, and she hugged me again.

"See, this is why you are perfect," Gina said, comfortingly.

It wasn't easy. But I had made mistakes in the past, and so now, at this point of my adulthood, doing what was right in regard to other people was something that was incredibly important to me. But right now, I wished I could just not worry about her feelings.

The rest of my workday was a blur as I focused on my clients, avoiding all thoughts about Vanessa, Peter, and my life.

When we closed the shop and headed out the door, Gina turned to me, "Do you want me to come over and hang out this evening? I don't want you to be alone unless you want to be. Tommy is out of town, and I don't have anything that I'm doing tonight, so I could sleep over?"

"Oh Gina," I replied, putting my arm around her. "I would absolutely love it if you came over tonight. You can go over plans with me, and we can have a cocktail or two."

"Or three," Gina replied, winking at me. "Let me run home and change and grab some clothes for tomorrow. I'll be over in like an hour or so."

"That sounds perfect. Yay!"

Our favorite cocktail was a spin off cucumber mint gimlet, so I stopped at the store for a few ingredients on my way home. I ran through the recipe in my mind. *Muddled cucumber and mint, gin, St. Germain, lime juice, and a dash of simple syrup. I need to grab some cucumbers for sure, and probably some more limes.*

There was a rush of emotion, and I could feel my throat choke up. Gina was really wonderful. It would have been a difficult night by myself alone with my thoughts, but now there'd be a few drinks and a lot of laughter.

I texted her, "I'm so glad you're coming over. You're the very bestest of friends, and I love you so much!"

"I love you too! Hey, I had a thought. We can talk it over when I get there, but have you ever considered talking to a life coach?"

I frowned and responded, "Do you think I need one? Isn't that just influencer nonsense?"

"My sister has one, and it's really helped her. I'll tell you about it when I get there. See you soon!" She sent with a few kissy faces and several martini emojis.

CHAPTER 4

"So, what are you trying to accomplish with this trip, Willa?" Gina asked.

I handed her the full martini glass and sat down next to her on my couch, my own glass in hand.

"I don't really know, to be honest." I replied. "Looking for my happiness, I guess?"

Gina frowned slightly, "I guess I didn't realize that you weren't happy? I mean, obviously this stuff with Peter is pretty heartbreaking, but other than that?"

I sipped my drink as I took a minute to think about how to respond to her question. "It's not that I'm unhappy, necessarily. It's more that I find myself discontent. Is this all that there is? Working, going out with friends, seeing my family… I mean, that's basically it - rinse and repeat week after week."

"Gina, I want a fairy tale life, as unrealistic as that might be," I continued. "One with magical moments and everything."

"I think everyone wants a fairy tale life, but I don't think that most people get them," she replied. "You know how much I love all things Disney, but I know that it isn't real."

"Well, why not? Why can't we have that life? I told my mom yesterday, it's not necessarily about finding a partner and living happily ever after. That would be cool and all, but for me right now, I just want magic. I want to be able to see the magic in the mundane and not just be depressed by the motions of life. I want to be able to break into song and dance at any moment just because life is beautiful."

Gina was smiling at me mischievously at the end of my rant. She grabbed her phone and clicked on something. "Like this?"

I listened as music started blaring from her phone and then laughed as I recognized "A Whole New World" from Aladdin.

She stood up and set her cocktail down on the end table. "Come," she motioned for me to join her, holding out her hands. With a little laugh, I complied.

We loudly sang along and danced to the whole song. Through the kitchen and around the island in the center of the room, collapsing back onto the couch laughing as it finished.

"So, just like that?" Gina asked, still laughing.

"Yes, dear. Just like that."

"Well, you don't need to go to the woods to do that. Just have a drink and turn on the Disney station."

"Very true." I replied, grinning at her.

"Anything to help! Seriously, though, I hear you on the 'magical out of the mundane.' There's lots of times I feel like I'm just going through the motions too."

"Yeah," I sighed. "But I don't know how it's going to change for me just by going into the woods. My mom said, 'life is simpler there' when she suggested it, but how does that help?"

"I don't know, but I guess you'll find out."

"Are you ready for another?" I asked, gesturing toward Gina's nearly finished glass.

"Girl! Of course I am!" she exclaimed.

I laughed and went over to the counter to make us both another. "So, tell me about your sister and her life coach. I really did think that was just like one of those influencer jobs that aren't really real."

"I know, but Denise came in last week for a keratin treatment and she was telling me that the one she is talking to is really helping."

"Helping her with what exactly?" I asked.

Gina hesitated, "We didn't really get into details, to be honest with you. Denise and I aren't really that close, and since we were talking about it at the salon, I didn't press for more."

"I don't really want anyone telling me how to live my life."

"I didn't get the impression that it's like that at all. From what I understand, her life coach is there for support and asks questions that help her figure things out on her own. It's more like passive guidance and accountability, I think."

"I guess that does sound helpful," I sighed, and added, "part of me feels like it's a weakness to have to ask someone to help. I know it isn't, but that's how it feels."

"I don't know babe, I was just thinking that maybe talking to someone could help. I don't know if it will, but maybe the life coach will have ideas about what to do or where to go."

"You're right, maybe it would. If I want things to change, I have to step outside my comfort zone, right?"

"Yes! I'll text Denise for the contact info, if you want?"

"Sure," I knew my response was not that enthusiastic, but the thought of talking to someone that was supposed to coach me through life felt like a blow to my pride. "Gina, am I actually that bad at life, and everyone else in the world is happy, and I'm the odd one out?"

Gina put down her phone. "No, love, you're the one brave enough to do something about it," Her tone was serious. "I guarantee that all of your friends, including me, will be piggy backing off of everything you learn."

"Okay," I replied. Then wanting to get out of this heavy conversation, "Want to look up Airbnbs?"

"I thought you'd never ask. Scrolling through Stays is one of my favorite pastimes." She grinned and scooted closer to me on the couch as I reached for my laptop.

"So, my mom mentioned the smoky mountains when she suggested this trip," I said, opening up Google Maps as well as Airbnb. A thought struck me, "Oh, you know what might be cool? Staying somewhere near the Appalachian Trail."

Gina clapped her hands, "Yes! I've always wanted to hike the Appalachian Trail."

"Me too," I agreed. "Maybe I can do a little stretch of it." I zoomed in to find the trail and followed it up into North Carolina. It crossed through a river in a town called Wesser.

"I bet that's beautiful. I'm going to try there."

Airbnb didn't have many options nearby, so I expanded my search. I scrolled through pictures, occasionally stopping to gawk at the especially beautiful ones. Gina got up to make us another drink.

She was shaking the martinis when I found it.

"Oh my god! Gina!" I squealed. "Come see. I found it. It's perfect."

"I'm coming," she responded with a laugh, pouring the cocktails into our glasses. She handed me mine and sat down, adjusting the laptop to face her. "Yes! I love A-frames."

We went through all the pictures again and read the description.

"Ooo, a hot tub!" Gina exclaimed. "I'm coming with you."

"I know, I can't wait for it. I can definitely find happiness in a hot tub," I replied, grinning.

"This house is just magical," Gina sighed as we finished. "The creek with its gazebo, and fire pit… you might just stay there forever."

I laughed. "I couldn't abandon you forever, dearest."

"Oh, you won't be abandoning me. I'd move in with you."

"What about Tommy?" I asked. I knew Gina's longtime partner had recently started his own trucking business, and was gone a lot these days.

"He won't mind. We'll build a cabin next to you when he finally gets to just do local runs."

We giggled. It was a lovely dream.

"Okay, so if you had to be a fairy tale princess, who would you be?" Gina asked, settling back into the couch.

"Hmmm. I'll have to think about that for a minute. Who would you pick?"

"Well, to be honest, it's not a princess."

"What? You can't go changing the rules already!" I exclaimed, laughing.

"Sure I can. But I guess I should have asked what fairy tale character... because I'd pick Peter Pan."

"Ooo that's such a good one."

"Yeah, it is, right? Forever young, I spend my days playing with my friends, and I can fly."

"I think flying would be my superpower," I replied, sidetracked.

"Oh, for sure, me too. Or maybe reading minds, I can't decide which I'd like more. But who is your fairy tale character?"

"Probably Rapunzel. Long glorious hair..." I shook my long curly mane at Gina, giggling, "trapped in a tower, longing to be free. Yeah, that's me right now."

"Oh, yes. That's perfect. But you're not waiting for a guy to come set you free, you're chopping off your hair and making a rope and going out to find the bears."

"All of the bears!" We were both laughing now.

Gina suddenly stopped laughing. "Willa, what if you do see a bear when you're out in the woods? You might get eaten. You'll be all by yourself and no one would know!"

"I'm not going to be eaten by bears, silly. I'll be in a magical place; bears don't eat the princesses."

"Wait, isn't there a fairy tale about that? The one where the princess gets kidnapped by the bear?"

"But it turns out he's actually a prince under a spell?" I asked. "Isn't it called East of the Sun West of the Moon? But I'm not sure that she was kidnapped. Didn't the bear ask her father or something?"

"I don't remember. It's only been like 30 years since I had to read that story for school." Gina protested. "I just remember that it was something about a bear and a princess. The question is, why do you remember it?"

"I don't know. It's one of the stories I remember my mom reading to me when I was little. I'm googling it," I replied, opening the laptop again.

Gina laughed, "Of course you are."

"Okay," I said, after skimming the results, "The bear asks her dad for her, and it turns out that he's a prince under a curse. His evil stepmother whisks him away to a castle East of the Sun and West of the Moon, so she hunts him down and they get married and live happily ever after."

"Of course they did," Gina sighed dramatically.

"So, see? I'm not going to get eaten by a bear. If I find one, it'll turn out to be a prince and we'll live happily ever after."

"Willa, if you find your forever guy up there… this will be the most romantic story of all time."

"Stop it. I'm not going to the woods to find myself a man. I'm going to find a happiness that isn't based on people, especially boys."

"I know, I know. But still. It could happen."

"You're such a romantic." I laughed.

"Yes, but you still love me."

"I do. Very much."

We smiled at each other and raised our glasses. "Cheers!" Gina exclaimed.

"Cheers! To best friends and happiness," I replied.

"Yes, indeed."

Our night was filled with laughter, but as we settled down to sleep, I found myself scrolling through my text messages. I clicked on the thread Peter and I were on and almost started a message telling him about my night with Gina. *What? You can't even go a half of a day without texting him?* Frustrated, I archived the thread so I wouldn't be as easily tempted to text him. *Effing Vanessa, ruining my world and stealing my best friend from me. This was going to really be the worst.*

I turned my phone over and closed my eyes, trying to shut off my brain. Gina had evidently not had much difficulty falling asleep because I could hear her rhythmic breathing coming through my open door. I listened for a little bit, quieting my mind and emotions by focusing on the sound. Before long, I too, was fast asleep.

CHAPTER 5

"Oh! My sister just texted me back," Gina told me the next morning. We were back at work and in between clients. "Here, I'm forwarding it to you."

I glanced at the incoming text, "Alright, I'll call her when I'm done with Lisa."

The app that we used to schedule clients had just notified me that Lisa had just checked in at the front desk.

Lisa was always a simple cut. I tried to fill the time with small talk, but my mind was freaking out about calling the life coach. *What would I even tell her? Was I supposed to tell her my life story? How was this person going to even help me? And why was I so scared to talk to someone?*

I didn't have any of those answers. I finished Lisa well before the allotted time and went into the back room to call before I chickened out.

"I actually had a cancellation this afternoon," the woman replied when I asked if I could set an appointment. "Would that work for you, or is that too soon? Otherwise, I'm pretty booked up until the end of next week."

"Oh wow!" I hesitated, if I waited until the end of next week to talk to this lady, I'd probably talk myself out of it. "Okay, yeah, what time?"

"Can you meet me at four at the Starbucks on 434?"

"Sure. That works." I didn't have any scheduled clients after three, and normally that would be when I would take walk-ins but, I could just leave when my last client was done. I gave her my name and number and told her that I would see her in a few hours.

I felt so rushed, though, as I hung up the phone. I should have asked her what the process was, but I'd been too nervous and too much in a hurry to get off the phone before someone came back.

Quit freaking out. I told myself, probably more harshly than needed. *This could be a good thing, you don't know.*

Gina looked at me questioningly as I left the back room. She was with a customer, so I just gave her a little smile and mouthed "I have an appointment."

She nodded back, her smile approving. She would have given me so much shit if I hadn't followed through with this.

Just before four, I walked into the Starbucks. The place was mostly empty besides a couple at one corner and a single woman in the other corner. She stood when I walked in.

"Willa?" she asked, coming towards me.

"Yes."

"I'm Christy, can I buy you a coffee?"

"Sure," I replied. We got in line and ordered our drinks.

"Is the corner table good for you?" she asked when our drinks were ready.

"Yeah, it's fine." The silence while we waited was a little awkward, but my first impression of her was favorable. She was probably fifteen years older than me, slightly graying. Her face was one of those that just seemed kind.

"So how does this work?" I asked as I sat down across from her.

Christy smiled and her eyes seemed to twinkle. "Don't worry, Willa. It's just a conversation. There's no pressure, and I'm not going to psychoanalyze you. A life coach isn't a therapist. I'm not going to try to fix you in any way, this initial meeting is just to get to know each other. We need to see if we mesh, if there are things that I can help you with, and for you to see if you can trust me to help you," She paused, then asked, "Would you like me to tell you my story first? Would that make you more comfortable?"

"Yes, please," I replied gratefully. It was hard to stay cautious when she had such a compelling smile and genuine warmth, but it would be easier to know what to tell her if I heard what she told me first.

"Well, I've always had a passion for people," she began, "though, my parents say that I started off by adopting animals first. Whenever I found an animal in the neighborhood - stray or not so much - I tried to bring it home with me."

Her smile was infectious, and I found myself smiling back at her.

"The older I got I started sort of adopting people instead. People with bad home lives gravitated toward me and I would bring them home to share my family with them. I really lucked out in having a big loving family and I just wanted to share that with people that needed it. I spent my college years working at restaurants, but I also volunteered doing an internship position for a local food pantry that worked with underprivileged families. We helped them with resources and food to get them back on their feet. I actually took it upon myself one year to provide a safe place for kids to come do their homework, get help, and have one on one time with people that listened and really cared. It went really well, but I ended up needing to do my own soul searching, so I left the project to do that."

Christy paused for a moment, obviously remembering. She continued after a moment, "Living an authentic life had become really important to me. I needed to make sure that the path I was on was the path that really spoke meaning and purpose from my heart into the world. So, I spent a few years traveling, meeting people all over the world and immersing myself in their cultures and beliefs. I wanted a greater understanding of people and what makes them tick, especially from cultures different than my own. I met my husband soon after I landed here in Orlando, it was just one of those chance things, but we became best friends and finally realized that life was just better together. We've been together going on 20 years now. He has brought such magic to my life that I never knew was possible." She smiled at me, I could tell she was thinking of her man. "Honestly, I don't think that I would have ended up doing this life coaching thing without him. It's so important to have people in your corner who believe you're capable of more than you think you are. Anyway, it's been really rewarding, seeing people making changes in their lives to become the person they've always wanted to be. Helping them work through the roadblocks and finding their path of purpose." She paused for a moment, and then asked, "What do you think? Would you be interested in sharing your story with me?"

"Yes," I replied, "I think I would. But do you mind if I ask you a question first?"

"No, of course not. Go ahead."

"Where do you find your happiness?"

"Hmmm," Christy leaned back in her chair, looking thoughtful. "I think that focusing on the moments is where happiness is found. Moments aren't usually bad, really. It's when I'm thinking about the past or the future that anxiety, despair, and depression can seep in. So if I have something negative going on in my life, I try to take myself out of it. Right here, right now, what is wrong? And then ask myself if it can be fixed right now. If that's not possible, then I try to notice my actions, my thoughts, and what's going on around me so that I stay in the moment. When the time comes that I can solve the problem, then I deal with it in the moment that it exists in."

I felt like I was staring blankly at her as she finished. Somehow her words felt like a foreign language.

"So basically, what you're saying is that you are happy when you are in the present and not allowing yourself to worry about the past or the future," I tried to summarize.

Christy laughed. "Yes! Sorry, I probably said that way too complicated."

"It's okay," I grinned back at her.

"So, I guess my final thoughts on happiness is that it relates a lot to how you feel about yourself. It's crucial to stop hating yourself for everything that you are not, and to start loving yourself for everything that you already are. It's also very important not to try to impress others. You are who you are and you've done what you've done. Be confident in who you are and who you want to be. Which brings me to my last point on this note: Don't ever give up on yourself. Give yourself goals, achievable goals, and as you finish them successfully, you'll build your confidence and self esteem. For me, tying all that in with helping others has given me what I like to call my happily ever after."

Christy's last words made me laugh out loud. If I had any doubts left that I wanted to work with her, those words made them vanish entirely.

"I'm not laughing at you, I promise," I explained hastily, "I'm just really glad you worded it like that. Can I tell you my situation now?"

"Please do." She took a sip of her coffee and sat back to listen.

I told her about my conversation with my mom, the further conversation with Gina, and then finally told her about Peter.

"Oh! I see why you liked my happily ever after." Christy exclaimed as I finished my story.

I laughed, "Yes. I'm the product of my generation with Disney culture and happily ever after's. Do you think I'm asking for too much? Is it possible to find my happily ever after if I don't have a man?"

"Of course it's possible. Everyone should find their happy, it makes any relationship you have so much better. So, no. You are not asking for too much. I would absolutely love to work with you on this! What do you think?"

I nodded. "I think so. Can I ask what it will look like though?"

"I set individual goals for each of my clients, we work towards them together, and chat as needed, but touch base at least once a week. For you, my initial thought is to have you definitely go to the woods like your mom suggested. We learn a lot about ourselves when we are alone, especially when we only give nature's rhythms a claim on our time."

"I want to believe you," I said, "especially because my mom said the same thing. I just don't see what difference it will make. I mean, I go out in nature here…"

"Part of it is making yourself uncomfortable." Christy's eyes seemed to twinkle again, I thought of Gina. Christy also seemed like she laughed easily. She was still talking so I made myself pay attention. "It's important to take yourself away from things that you feel are normal. We grow when we step outside our comfort zones."

"That makes sense. I guess I'll check my schedule and book the Airbnb I found."

"Oh good. If I can make a suggestion?"

"Please do," I replied.

"I would try to be spontaneous with this trip. Do lots of exploring. Talk to the people you meet along the way. Try asking everyone where they find their happiness."

CHAPTER 6

Christy and I left the coffee shop a little while later. Before we parted ways I had set up another appointment with her for the end of next week. She said that we could do it in person or via video chat depending on what ended up being best for my schedule.

"She seems great," I texted Gina, as I got home. "She agreed with my mom that I should go to the woods, so I'm going to book that Airbnb now."

"I'm so glad!" came her response. "With Tommy, talk tomorrow."

"Okay!" I sent a few kissy faces and a wink and grinned to myself. She and Tommy were so cute. They had such limited time together these days that they really gave each other quality time whenever they could.

I settled onto my couch and pulled up my saved list on Airbnb. I scrolled through the pictures again, excited at the prospect of staying here. I clicked on the available dates and my excitement suffered a blow. Only 2 nights were available in the next month and a half, and those days were next week.

Could I go next week? My bookings are so full right now. I opened my calendar. Maybe I could rearrange things so that it would be possible. Mother's Day would be past, and we'd be in graduation season. I'd have to make a few calls and pawn off the ones who couldn't adjust. Of course I could just book a different house, but I really wanted to stay here. Something about it just seemed to call to me.

I clicked Book Now.

The days had felt so long as I waited to leave. I called Christy and told her that I had booked the place in North Carolina. She was excited for me and asked that we schedule our video chat for the day after my arrival up there. I agreed, happier than I thought that I would be, even knowing that she'd have some things for me to do.

We hadn't even done anything yet, and I already felt like I would be able to figure out my happily ever after. Maybe it was the house, maybe it was doing something outside of my norm. I didn't know.

I had spent hours researching the area to see what would be around and what my options were for things to do. There were a lot of different trails not too far away from the house, and really, what better way to spend time in the woods than going for some hikes? But I wasn't an experienced hiker by any stretch of the imagination. This was definitely going to be an adventure.

If I decided to stay longer, there were several hotels or other AirBnB options, even campgrounds around, so I was bringing along a sleeping bag and a hammock with a tent option just in case.

I walked down the steps of my condo, my new small hiking backpack on my back.

Oh my god. I can't believe I'm actually doing this! A little bit scared but mostly excited, I tossed the backpack in the backseat of my car.

I snapped a quick selfie and sent it to Gina. "I'm on my way! Wish me luck and pray I don't die lol".

"Don't even say that!" She sent back immediately. "Be safe, but have so much fun! I hope you come home with all of the answers you're looking for."

I set my phone down and started my car. The radio came on with the car and Tom Petty was singing Wildflowers.

I grinned. So perfect.

I pulled out my phone again and texted Peter.

"I'm headed off on my adventure! Hope you're doing well, and can't wait to catch up when I get back."

I'd been so good about not texting him this whole week, but it had definitely been a struggle.

"Back at ya! Be careful!" came his response.

I looked at it for a minute trying to decide whether or not to say anything else. I just wanted more. I wondered if he'd missed me this whole time we hadn't texted. Probably not, Vanessa would be filling the void. I sighed and put down the phone. I turned up the music and backed out of my parking spot.

The drive up to Saluda, North Carolina, where my cabin was, had an ETA of eight hours seventeen minutes, projected arrival time 5:30 p.m. if I didn't stop too much. Well, I wasn't planning on it. I'd downloaded a book on Audible to listen to when I got bored of the radio. But right now, the radio turned up and the wind in my hair, driving down the freeway, did it really get much better than this?

By the time I stopped for a late lunch my mind had created a million different scenarios for how this adventure was going to go. *Was I going to be alone the whole time? Would I even see other people? Why was this thought so intimidating? I live alone, I should be fine. But I also see people every day, whether it's a work day and I hang out with Gina and the other girls in our small salon, or a day off and I'm at my parents house or out with Peter or our other friends.*

Was I just going to go dance in the woods by myself and magically find this happiness my mom was certain that I would find? Was I supposed to treat this like a vacation and just do things for myself while I was gone, or was this more of a mission to figure out happiness? Christy has some ideas, I know, but what will they be?

I sighed heavily. I needed a distraction. I still had 2 more hours left according to the GPS. The radio wasn't coming through with a great selection of music now that I was getting into the mountains, so I turned on my audio book.

"It Is What You Make of It" by Justin McRoberts had been a suggested title on my recommended list. I had read the synopsis and it sounded like a book that would certainly fit in with what I was trying to do. I turned it on, hoping that listening to it would quiet my brain.

The book started playing and I found myself enthralled. The author told his stories in a humorous but genuinely real way, and so many of the things he mentioned really touched my soul.

When I finally drove up the driveway, I could see that the cabin was everything I had hoped it would be. Town had only been about ten minutes away, but I was up the mountain and it felt like there was no one around for miles. *So many trees to get lost in, but first… I* thought, as I parked and stepped out of my car. *First, I want to see this house and hot tub. Luxury awaits!* I grinned, it was going to feel so good to soak in a hot tub after that long drive.

I walked up the stairs to the door. *Should I video everything so that I could share this experience with my mom and Gina, and maybe even Peter? I wish he was here with me.* I thought, and then just as quickly, *Stop. Stop thinking about him. He's happy. Do this for yourself.*

I left my phone in my pocket, deciding that this adventure of mine was going to be mine alone. *I'll take pictures later to remember it, but maybe I could try for a cellphone-less experience on this trip?* The thought was a little daunt-ing, but… *Disney princesses in the woods never had phones.* I chuckled to myself, imagining the story of Rapunzel if she'd had a phone.

The key to the cabin was in a lockbox on the side of the door. The owner had given me the combination in an email, so I pulled it up and opened the door.

I gasped. The log cabin interior was beautiful. The pictures hadn't done it justice at all. It was perfect, the edges were framed with little fairy lights, and it seemed like there was greenery everywhere. There was a note on the table with my name on it.

I opened it and read, *"Dear Willa, We hope you have a wonderful stay in our mountain home. I know you said that you were excited about using the hot tub after your long drive, so I had it uncovered and turned on for you. If there is anything you need, please don't hesitate to call. There are brochures for local activities on the side table next to the couch if you need ideas. Enjoy your stay!"*

My hand was on my heart as I finished reading the note. How precious of them! I set the note back down and went through the house to the back porch where the hot tub sat. Opening the sliding glass door, my jaw dropped again, everything was in bloom. Pinks, reds and yellows, and the bright greens of spring. It had felt like summer in Florida for a few weeks now, so it was such a strange feeling to be up here where spring was new again. The backyard tran-sitioned into the wooded mountain-scape towards the back, but as I looked to the right, I could see down the mountain and glimpse the valley below. The view was indescribably incredible. I couldn't wait to relax in the hot tub and just immerse myself in the wonder of it.

I went back out to the car to grab my things and noticed the hammock set up by the gazebo in the side yard. *There is the creek with its small footbridge crossing the banks!* I smiled, if I had to pick my perfect spot, this would be it.

I went inside and up the stairs to the loft where the bed was. It had such a bohemian aesthetic, something that was very much my style preference. I felt so full of excitement, joy, and wonder. Those feelings had been in such short supply lately. Though, the more I thought about it, it wasn't just lately, it was pretty much since I had become an adult. *Why is it only kids that have those feelings on a regular basis? It shouldn't be like that, right? I'm so glad Mom suggested this getaway. It's going to be wonderful.*

I unpacked my clothes and put my toiletries in the adjacent bathroom. *Bikini time!* I changed and went out the back door again, breathing in the fragrant smells of the blooming yard. Turning on the jets, I stepped up into the hot tub and sat down with a sigh. Perfection.

I sat there for a few minutes, enjoying the jets of hot water, and then I reached for my phone and turned on my audible book. It was about halfway finished, and like I had thought, it was right in line with what I had been needing, especially as I began this adventure. I set my phone down on the shelf and closed my eyes. I let myself relax into the water, the author's voice rhythmic and soothing.

CHAPTER 7

It was before dawn when I woke up the next morning. I could see the sky was just starting to lighten up as I looked out of the skylight above me. I crashed early last night after settling in from my time in the hot tub. The skylight above my bed had revealed a sky full of stars that hadn't been visible back home in Florida. This morning, though, the stars could no longer be seen as the sky brightened with the dawn. I turned over, snuggling one of the pillows. Such a magical evening. That book had inspired me, and I couldn't wait to tell Christy about it. It made me determined now not to allow myself a life resigned to "it is what it is," but I would create something beautiful from the moments. I was going to have to buy the real book to re-read when I got home.

I grabbed my phone and googled "coffee near me", but nothing was open yet, so I went downstairs to see if there was a coffee maker in the kitchen. I hadn't noticed yesterday, but I breathed a sigh of relief when I saw it there on the counter, next to a grinder. A small basket sat next to it with a few different bags of coffee beans in it and another note. "Happy Mug Coffee is the best roaster we've ever found, they might not be local to North Carolina, but it's a delicious coffee. We leave a few bags for our guests, so please feel free to take it with you when you leave."

I picked up a bag of dark roast, the little caricature of a coffee mug caught my fancy right away. It was so original. I opened the bag and breathed in the aroma. *Oh my god. It smells like heaven!*

A few minutes later, I was out on the back porch again, coffee in hand. The cool mountain air was a little bit chilly for my Floridian blood, but it was so refreshing. I sat on the hammock-style porch swing and closed my eyes. The birds were just waking up too, and I could hear the twitters and songs in the silence of the morning. Everything was just so quiet, no ambient sounds of traffic, no distant sirens, just birds with their songs and occasional flutter of wings.

This is happiness. I thought, blissful. *Maybe I should get a notebook and write down when I have moments like this, maybe this is what my mom meant. But could it be that simple? Quiet mornings with truly amazing coffee is the key to happiness?* I asked myself as I took another sip. I smiled. *Right now? Yes. Yes, it is.*

The sun came up, lighting up the sky with its many shades of pinks and reds coloring the wispy clouds. I found myself hardly even thinking, just enjoying the view and my coffee, watching the birds and the squirrels in the yard.

My phone vibrated, and I nearly jumped out of my skin. *Who on earth would be calling me this early? Oh shit. Mom.*

"Hey, did you make it up there okay?"

"Yeah, Mom, I'm sorry I forgot to text you. The drive was uneventful, but I'm here and the house is so perfect."

"Okay, good. I don't want to disturb you, I was just a little bit worried since I hadn't heard anything from you."

"Yeah, everything is good. I'm on the back porch drinking coffee in a hammock swing, listening to the birds. It's definitely happiness."

"I'm glad, baby. Don't forget to check in from time to time. I don't want to hear that you got eaten by bears."

I giggled, remembering the laughter with Gina. "I'm not going to get eaten. Gina said that too, but then she decided that the bear was going to turn into a handsome prince, and we'd live happily ever after."

"Okay…" I could hear the laughter in her voice, "I'm not sure how I feel about bear princes… but, okay. Be safe. Love you."

"I will. I love you, too."

I put down my phone and took another sip from my coffee mug.

I hadn't packed any food except granola bars, so when my stomach started growling, I knew it was time to look up breakfast places nearby. *A grocery store would probably be a good idea too.* There were a couple breakfast places in town and they all had good reviews, so I put my phone away and decided to just wing it. Everything seemed open by now, so whichever I came across first would suit me just fine.

I swept up my long curly hair into a high ponytail and tried to tuck my flyaways behind my ear. They refused to be tamed, though, so I gave up and got dressed. I chose a sleeveless pale blue blouse and white shorts. *Not exactly a Disney princess, but not bad.* I thought as I walked up to the mirror to put on my mascara. Blues, greens, and whites were my go-to colors when it came to clothes because they suited my hair and complexion so well. *But who am I trying to impress? The bears?* I giggled to myself.

I drove around the little town for a bit before stopping. There were a few antique shops and tourist shopping spots, but all I needed was breakfast at this point. A cafe on the corner looked cute, so I stopped and went in. I sat myself near the window and looked around. There weren't many empty tables, and it took a minute for the server to come over.

"I'm so sorry, it's been a crazy morning," she apologized, as she handed me the menu.

"There's no rush, I totally understand," I smiled back at her sympathetically. I understood. I had waited tables for a while before I went to cosmetology school.

"Can I get you a coffee or orange juice?"

"I already had my coffee this morning, but an orange juice and a water would be perfect, thank you."

She nodded and dashed off. There were two older women seated at the table next to me, so I looked to see what they were eating. Just tea and a muffin, apparently. One of them noticed my glance and smiled at me.

"Everything here is homemade. Evie and I come here at least once a week to get one of these morning glory muffins."

"That's awesome. I'm only in town for a few days, but I'm excited to have found this spot. It's so cute in here," I replied, looking around the cafe again. The wall of books was surrounded by lots of windows and natural light, and the interior colors of whites and browns just felt happy.

"Well, welcome! Where are you from?"

"Orlando."

"Wow! That's far. What brings you to our mountains?"

"I'm on a quest," I laughed. "I don't know how to explain it really, but I'm trying to figure out happiness, how to have a joy that comes from within and isn't based on people or circumstances. My mom suggested that I might find the answers I'm looking for in the woods, so here I am."

The women were smiling at me as I finished.

"I think that's just wonderful, dear." The woman called Evie replied, "I think more people should go on quests of that sort."

"Oh yes indeed." The other woman agreed. "I think the woods are a great place to start. Have you come up with anything so far?"

"Sort of. I'm going to get a notebook so I can process and write everything down. Yesterday as I was driving up here…"

I paused as the waitress came back with my orange juice and water. "Can I get the frittata with potatoes, please?"

"We have a spinach and mushroom one or ham and cheese?"

"Ham and cheese."

"I'll get that right in for you," she replied.

"Thank you." I turned back to the ladies, "I'm sorry."

"No, it's fine. Continue though, you were saying that yesterday when you were driving up here…"

"Oh, yeah, I was listening to a book that really spoke to me about life being what you make of it instead of the attitude that 'it is what it is.' And then this morning I was sitting out on the back deck drinking coffee and listening to the birds as the sun came up. There was just such a peaceful serenity that I felt like happiness was just bubbling inside of me. And I know this sounds silly, but even in this cafe, the vibe is just happy, too."

The women smiled, delighted at the compliment to their cafe.

"That's amazing," the one whose name I didn't know responded.

"I think you're well on your way, dear," Evie rejoined. "And I totally agree with you about this place. It is happy in here."

"Do you have any suggestions for this quest of mine?" I had remembered that Christy had told me to ask the people I met on this trip about their versions of happiness. But I wasn't sure yet how to pose the question. Besides, I didn't want to intrude too much on their breakfast.

Both women looked thoughtful. "Well, I think gratitude has been the key for me in my life." The one responded after a moment, "When I can look around myself with appreciation, and even awe, I find that my happiness is easily found. So, I guess my advice is to be thankful as much as possible. Even when things are tough, look for the simple things, even if it's just lungs that work, or eyes that see. Remind yourself of these things when your happiness feels distant."

"That's beautiful. Thank you."

The waitress came back with my food and set it down. "Is there anything else I can get you?"

"No, thank you."

She turned around to the ladies as I opened my silverware and took a bite.

"Ladies, is there anything else I can get for you today?"

"No, dear, we're leaving now. I hope you have a wonderful day," Evie responded.

The waitress nodded, "Ya'll too. See you next week."

The women gathered up their things and turned back to me.

The one whose name I hadn't caught said, "I hope you have a wonderful stay here and find everything that you're looking for."

"Yes," Evie agreed, "I think what you're doing is just wonderful, and I'm glad to know that there are people like you in the world."

I was blushing at the obvious sincerity in their voices. "Thank you so much. It was my honor to get to talk to you both."

Evie patted my hand as she walked past me. "You're a blessing, child."

"So are you."

I focused on my food as they left. This frittata was amazing. Those women had been so overwhelmingly kind. *It's crazy how different, and kinder, people are outside of the city.* My heart felt full once again, and I almost felt like crying. This was starting off to be such a beautiful adventure.

CHAPTER 8

Back at my temporary mountain home, I settled into the hammock. I had found a notebook at one of the shops downtown that would suit my purposes. The nearby creek, gazebo, and firepit made this a perfect spot to sit and enjoy my surroundings. I had wanted to find magic, and here it was, just for me. I sighed contentedly and opened the notebook, pen in hand.

"The Happiness Quest "

I titled it, giggling a little bit to myself.

Lessons Learned

1. It is what you make of it, "it is what it is" is a cop out. Building something with what you've been given, and with the people you have in your life, will give you a sense of purpose and fulfillment. Waiting for something to happen without moving in a direction is a recipe for unhappiness.

2. Quiet mornings listening and watching nature (and drinking delicious coffee) have some sort of magic too. I have a feeling I'll discover more in this vein.

3. Gratitude and Awe are instrumental in finding happiness within you, according to my old ladies at the café - the awe that I feel here, and the thankfulness that I was able to get this house, even if it's just for a few days - makes me inclined to think that they know what they're talking about.

I closed the book.

I lay there for a few minutes listening to the creek. *Peter would love it here. He had talked fondly about his life in the country when he was a kid, finding crawdads in the creek. I wonder if there's crawdads in the creeks here?* I sighed. *Okay, no more thinking about Peter.* I told myself firmly.

But my brain didn't listen to me. I lay there for a few minutes just thinking and opened the notebook again.

4. Missing your favorite person can have adverse effects… and thinking about it feels like coming down from this joy high that I've been riding all morning. What do I do now?

I closed the notebook again and got out of the hammock. Sitting still just wasn't going to work for me right now. I would get depressed if I sat still much longer. I went back into the house and pulled out the fluffy princess dress that I'd brought with me. The video for Gina was going to happen. My zoom call with Christy was scheduled for later this afternoon, but I would have plenty of time.

The dress I had brought with me was a pale mint green that I had worn for a wedding several years before. It had been a princess theme, so all the bridesmaids had worn ball gowns in different shades. I had kept mine for no good reason other than it was beautiful. The green with my red hair and skin tone looked amazing. It had a sweetheart neckline with capped sleeves, a corset waist, and yards of fluff for the high-low skirt. There was never going to be another occasion to wear it, but now I was glad that I still had it.

I turned on the Disney station while I got ready, singing along as I combed out my long wavy hair, embracing my inner Rapunzel.

It didn't take me long to put on the dress and get my hair to cooperate in some fashion. Down with a light twist on either side of my head and joined in the back in a fancy clip.

Okay, I studied myself in the mirror. *That should work. Oh wait. I should make a flower crown with some of the flowers outside. That will be perfect!*

I turned away and went to grab my phone. *Where should I film this? I have to do it in the woods, so doing it in the yard won't work. I could just walk up the mountain further, but I don't know whose property that is. And what if it's hunting season? I'll just go out on one of the trails nearby.* I pulled open the trails app and picked one that said moderate and ran along the river. The reviews for the trail said to bring along a swimsuit, just in case you feel like jumping in. This plan for my afternoon was sounding better and better. Hopefully since it was a weekday there wouldn't be many other people on the trail to stare at my ridiculous hiking attire. I laughed softly to myself. *So what if they did stare, they'll laugh, I'll laugh. This is a happiness adventure after all.*

I tossed my swimsuit and towel in my small day bag and grabbed a bottle of water. I headed out to the back yard to collect some flowers for my flower crown, realizing I hadn't made one of these since I was a little kid. Another thing to add to the notebook. *Embracing your inner child definitely enhances happiness.* I eyed the flowers around me to see what would work best in the flower crown. Along the edges of the yard were the flowers that I wanted. Yellow Buttercups, little white flowers whose name I wasn't sure of, and the brilliant purplish blues of the Bluets. Once upon a time I had thought about becoming a florist and had studied a few books on flowers. I didn't remember all of them, but some had stuck with me. I gathered a handful of what I would need for my crown and went to sit by the firepit while I braided them together.

I couldn't stop smiling as I put it on my head and got into the car, this was the funniest and probably the craziest thing I'd ever done.

It was only a fifteen minute drive to the trailhead, and I was thankful to see that there were no other cars in the parking area. I adjusted my dress that had gotten slightly mushed while driving, grabbed my bag, and started down the trail.

The path wasn't very intense, so I found myself focusing on little things around me. A cricket jumped ahead of my footsteps, also keeping to the path. *I wonder how far crickets travel in their lifetime. Does he know that I'm not chasing him?* I stopped for a moment at that thought, and the cricket jumped off the path.

I adjusted my pack and kept on walking, enthralled by the beauty around me. The trail was lined with pink and white mountain laurel. The green moss growing on fallen trees and huge rocks made this area picture perfect. It felt like my heart was in my throat as I walked along. I hadn't realized natural beauty would affect my emotions this much. I turned a curve around a huge boulder that had been obscuring the view and gasped. To my left the river flowed with a steady roar. I was accustomed to the quiet rivers that flowed from the springs near my home in Florida. This river was so much louder as it crashed over rocks and boulders. To my right, the land flattened, and the trees thinned out. Forest flowers were blooming everywhere. A large, flattened rock was positioned next to a tree with a smaller trail leading to it. Obviously other people had gone to sit on this rock also, but for now, it was all mine. I walked over and set my pack down beside the rock, embracing the wonder that was overflowing from my heart. This was such an unfamiliar but also such a wonderful feeling. *I wonder if it's possible to keep this feeling? This is the magic that I was hoping to find. This is the feeling that I was looking for. I really do feel like I really could just sing and dance with the forest creatures like all the fairy tale characters.* As if in response to my thought, a robin swooped down from the trees and landed near me, twittering enthusiastically.

"Hello little fella," I said, "Are you happy today too?"

He cocked his head at me at the sound of my voice. I laughed.

Maybe he would join in the video, Gina would be in raptures if that happened. I thought with another giggle.

He flew up into a nearby tree, and I got out my phone to figure out the best spot for the video. I was able to lean my phone against the tree and stepped back into the clearing. I wracked my brain trying to think of the perfect song. The one that I kept coming back to was "Colors of the Wind" from Pocahontas. It seemed like the only song that was appropriate for the woods, plus, I knew all the words. I turned on the music on my phone and hummed along as I situated my flower crown that was already starting to wilt a little bit. I reset the music and made sure that I'd be visible in the video, then hit record. It felt a little awkward at first, dancing alone, spinning around the trees, but by the time I was singing the end of the second line, it was just right.

I finished the last note to the song, twirling around one more time. I started to reach for my phone to shut off the video but heard a noise behind me. It was clapping. I spun around, mortified. A woman stood by the boulder that had blocked the view of this clearing from the path.

"I'm sorry, I didn't mean to scare you," she said penitently, as she walked up the little path toward me.

"I wasn't expecting an audience," I replied, my face still flaming with embarrassment.

"Well, you have nothing to be self-conscious about. That was so great."

"I've wondered what it would be like to dance and sing in the forest," she continued, "like in all the Disney movies. I'm really happy that I've now seen someone actually do it."

"Really? You have?" I asked her, surprised.

She grinned back at me, "Well, maybe just this time. But honestly, it really seemed like such a perfectly natural thing to come across on such a beautiful day in this little clearing. I swear, I'm half convinced you're just pretending to be a human, you're probably a fairy or something."

I giggled at the thought. "It's possible."

"I don't want this magic to disappear, so I'm going to leave you to it," she said, "Continue your fairy magic, I'm off to the swimming hole at the end of the trail."

"Have fun!" I called after her.

"Oh!" She turned back, "if you see a big bear of a man, that's my brother. Tell him he's a slow poke, and I got tired of waiting on him."

I laughed, "Okay."

I sat down on the rock and watched the video I had recorded. It was hilarious. I hadn't been able to stop the recording before being startled by the clapping, so watching me jump out of my skin at the end had me laughing until tears came. *Not quite the finish I wanted, but this is going to be a great story for Gina. She is going to die laughing.* I thought, still smiling.

I grabbed my pack, then hesitated. *I don't really want to follow that girl.* I realized. It was one thing being alone, but quite another knowing that she and her brother were going to be at the swimming hole. Especially since she had seen me singing and dancing like a crazy person. *Besides, it's too cold to swim right now.* My Florida blood protested at swimming below 80 degrees, and this air near the river was certainly way colder than that.

I turned away from my spot and headed back down the trail the way I had come. Turning the corner of the rock, I saw a man approaching in the distance. He was a big man, and I could immediately see why his sister had referred to him as a bear of a man. As he neared me, I smiled, I could now tell Gina that I had found a bear on the trail. He was easily 6'5", I guessed, and built like a wrestler.

He looked at me quizzically, a grin brightening up his face. "What are you dressed for? A fairy conclave?"

"I wish," I laughed, "I met your sister, she said to tell you that she couldn't wait for you. She might have called you a slow poke."

He let out a hearty laugh. "She's a brat. I better catch up to her. Have a good day!"

"You too," I said, as I stood aside for him to pass me on the trail.

I continued my way down the trail, with a brief glance back over my shoulder at the back of the large man. I had often wished for a sibling, and this brother and sister exchange, the humor they possessed, made me a little bit jealous.

CHAPTER 9

I got back to the cabin with a little bit of time to spare before my video chat with Christy. I found my notebook out on the hammock swing on the back deck and settled in to refresh my mind of the things I had written down so far. I'd tell her those things, and of course I'd tell her about today's adventure in the woods.

I made a new entry:

5. Embracing your inner child

The silliness of making myself a flower crown, dressing up, and pretending to be a Disney princess, is so ridiculous. The adult in me scoffs and thinks the whole thing is stupid. But there is another part of me that just revels in it. That part thinks it was the most fun I've had in years. Maybe I should silence the fun sucking adult, and do the fun things more often.

I logged into the zoom meeting and smiled at Christy as she appeared.

"So, how is it?" she asked after we exchanged greetings.

"Just beautiful. I'm so glad you added your encouragement for me to do this. Can I read you some of the things I've written down?"

"Of course. I'd love to hear."

Her smile was so big by the time I finished. "I love that you're writing everything down!" she exclaimed, "Don't stop."

"I just thought that it would be the best way for me to remember everything and process the things that I hopefully learn on this trip," I replied.

"You're so right. When you come home we can go over everything, but let's talk more about what you're feeling now?"

I thought for a moment. "Honestly, Christy, I've had several moments already that have made me feel that happily ever after feeling that I was missing. They don't seem to last indefinitely, though, but I really think I've only scratched the surface so far."

She nodded. "I agree."

"Your suggestion of talking to people," I continued, "has been great. I wish I had talked more to the ladies about gratitude. But maybe it will come up again."

"I'm sure it will. My suggestion is that you keep on adventuring and talking to people. But make sure you're leaving time to just be quiet in the woods too. Especially if you find yourself near water. Let your body relax into the speed of things around you."

I had no idea what she meant by that, but I decided that I would just try anyway. If I couldn't figure it out, I'd ask later.

"Have you decided how long you're going to be gone yet?" Christy asked.

"Not really. I'm just going to wing it. I have this place for another day, and then I was thinking I'd go exploring. I think doing a hike on the Appalachian Trail should happen at the very least. I'll adjust my clients as needed."

"I'm really proud of you, Willa. You're diving into this with such determination."

I felt my face flush. "Yeah, I guess I am. I just really need to figure this out."

"Well, I have no doubt that you will."

We ended the call, and I headed out to the grocery store. Kabobs on the grill and s'mores over the fire were on the agenda for the evening.

The next morning I found myself drinking coffee in the swing on the back porch again. Once again, the peace and quiet and beauty of the morning were incomparable. But I also noticed that there was restlessness too. Besides the very few interactions yesterday, I hadn't talked to anyone or even got on my phone. *There's no reason I should feel so lonesome, or feel like I'm the only person left in the world, but, damn. I think it's just the solitude and quiet.* I mused, making myself get up.

I went back to the same cafe I had enjoyed so much yesterday. Walking in the door, I noticed one of the women I had talked to. It was the one whose name I hadn't caught. She saw me too and waved.

"I was hoping that you were going to come in today!" she exclaimed, as I neared her to say hello.

"Well, here I am." I responded, "I was thinking about making breakfast at the house this morning, but I realized I needed to make sure that I was not the only human left on Earth after basically 24 hours in the silence of the woods. I know, I'm such a city girl." My tone was rueful at the end.

"Don't feel like that," the woman responded, kindly. "That's a perfectly normal feeling to have when you're unaccustomed to quiet. Here, sit with me, please."

I sat down across from her. "I'm so sorry, I don't think I caught your name yesterday."

"Oh, I'm sorry dear, my name is Rita. I didn't get your name either."

"It's Willa," I smiled back at her. "I'm happy you were here today, it's good to see a friendly face."

"Yes. Yes, it is. So, I spent the rest of the day yesterday thinking about this happiness quest that you're on."

"Did you really?" I asked, surprised.

"Yes! I think it's just wonderful!" she exclaimed. "Do you have plans for what you're going to do on this adventure?"

"Not really," I confessed, "I only have the house until tomorrow. It was only available for these three days, so I was thinking I might do some hiking and camping, maybe go out to the Appalachian Trail. I'm not sure. It looks like there's a lot to explore out here, especially if I want to immerse myself in the woods."

"Well, the reason I was hoping that you were going to be here this morning is because I wanted to invite you to my house for dinner tonight. My niece and nephew are visiting, they're about your age, and I think you all might have a good deal in common. They're just passing through on a hiking trip also."

I hesitated before answering, *A stranger was inviting me to her house for dinner. That's weird, right? But...* "Sure, I'd love to come." I heard myself saying.

"Oh, I'm so glad," Rita beamed, and I found my doubts subsiding. She certainly didn't seem like a serial killer.

The waitress came over and I ordered a muffin and a tea since Rita had so highly recommended them yesterday.

"Have you always lived here?" I asked, after the waitress had left.

"No, no. I'm from Nebraska originally, but my husband and I moved here when we retired. He's gone now, but I love it here, it's very different from the plains. We have a wonderful little community and I have friends like Evie to keep me company. William and I never had kids, but my niece and nephew are like my own."

"Do your niece and nephew live in Nebraska then?"

"No, my niece is married and lives in Richmond, and my nephew lives in Savannah. Normally my niece's husband comes also, but he's out of town on business and so it's just Emily and Damien coming to visit this time."

"That's nice, I'm sure you'll enjoy your time with them. Are you sure you want me to invade your family time?"

"Oh yes! Definitely. My niece and nephew are both avid hikers and know these mountains very well, so I'm sure they'll have suggestions for your adventure. But not only that, their lives are also ones that I think you'll appreciate."

"Now I'm really intrigued!" I exclaimed.

"Good," she responded, smiling widely. "I know it must feel weird to come over to a stranger's house for dinner and meet my family, but hopefully this will pique your interest enough to get you past that."

"Yes. It has, for sure."

The waitress came back with my muffin and tea.

"Tell me more about you, Willa," Rita encouraged. "What is your life like?"

I took a sip from the steaming mug. *Delicious.*

"Well, I'm 34, never been married. I'm a hair stylist in Orlando. Hmm, I've done a little bit of traveling, but most of my life has been spent in that area. My father passed away years ago, so it's just my mom and me. I live about ten minutes away from their house, so I spend a lot of time with her," I paused to think. "What else? I go to trivia nights with my best friends pretty regularly, but that's about it. I know, it's so boring."

"I'm sure there's much more to you than that little summary. I doubt very much that you are boring," Rita responded, kindly. "Do you have a boyfriend… or girlfriend?"

"No," I said, my heart twinging a little as I thought of Peter. "I have a guy best friend, and honestly, I always thought we'd turn into something, but he told me recently that he's in love. So that's been a little rough adjusting to. I have to admit it's been nice to be able to run away into the mountains. I'll have to meet her when I get back to town, but right now, I am getting used to not talking to him every day."

"Oh, honey. I'm sorry. I'm sure that's been hard for your heart."

"Yes, it has," I said, thoughtfully. "I didn't realize how much I had expectations in that direction until it was taken off the table."

"Expectations are the root of most unhappiness for sure," she replied, ruefully. "I've had that come back to bite me several times during the course of my life."

"Ohhhh, I'm going to have to think about that," I wanted some time to process what she just said and figure out if it was true. "I did buy a notebook yesterday and started writing in it. I've titled it "**The Happiness Quest**" and hopefully by the end it will be full of the things I've learned."

Rita laughed delightedly. "That's wonderful. I'm going to have to tell Evie, she'll love it. You'll have to share it with us when you're done."

The conversation flowed easily as we exchanged stories from our lives. Rita and her husband had traveled the world extensively because of his job, but now her life was a quiet one. I got the impression though that she was satisfied. It seemed like she had done and experienced the things she had wanted to and was happy with how her life had played out. *I hope I'm the same way when I am old.*

When I got home to the cabin, I found I was still thinking about what Rita had said about expectations. I wanted to write it all down, so I grabbed my notebook and went to lay in the hammock.

I re-read the entry from yesterday and then continued with more thoughts.

6. Expectations. I guess if I'm honest, I think almost every time I've been unhappy it's been because I had expectations that were unfulfilled. I wanted something and because I didn't get it, my happiness was gone. How do I manage my expectations to prevent that from happening? I don't want to be ambivalent about things. Hopefully I can get further clarification on this during this adventure.

I should have talked to her about gratitude too, and asked about her experiences with expectations. I'll just see if it comes up at dinner tonight, I guess. I closed the notebook.

The sun was bright and warm, but not overwhelming like the sun in Florida. The partial shade provided by the trees and the light breeze made this perfect hammock weather. I found myself just watching the birds and squirrels flit along the branches of the trees above me, vaguely wondering about their lives and what they were doing.

My thoughts drifted to Peter as they tended to do when my mind got quiet, I was thinking of him less and less in the few weeks that we had gone without talking. I was realizing that I did miss him, but the shattered dream of eventually being together didn't plague me. I had never had a friend like him before, our late night conversations had led to him knowing me better than anyone had ever even tried to know me in the past, and vice versa. I didn't want to lose that, and it hurt to think that would change. There was such a safety in being known and being loved for who you truly are. But, if I took out the expectations of the future out of the equation, and looked back at what was, I could only feel thankfulness. It was a special connection, one of the rarest, and I was lucky enough to have had it in my life. *It's crazy how gratitude really does change your whole perspective.*

CHAPTER 10

I was second guessing my decision to go to Rita's house by the end of the afternoon. It felt weird to not only be intruding on family time, but also a family of strangers. I felt more comfortable with her now after our conversation at the cafe this morning, but adding in her niece and nephew felt intimidating.

I'm not bailing, though. I told myself fiercely, as I made myself get ready. *This adventure is about pushing past my normal reservations. It could be great.*

Rita had given me the address to her house, situated just outside the downtown area, so I pulled up just after five. Taking a deep breath, I knocked on the door of the quaint little house.

I heard steps coming to the door and took a step back as the door opened.

"Oh, it's you!" I exclaimed involuntarily. The open door had revealed the bear-like man from the trail.

"It's you too!" He laughed, "I'm Damien." He held the door open for me and I stepped inside blushing. Rita hurried over to us.

"Willa, welcome!" She greeted me. "This is my nephew, Damien." She paused and looked at us questioningly as she noticed my blushing face and Damien's chuckle. "Did I miss something?"

"Not at all, Auntie," Damien replied, the laughter still in his voice. "Willa and I met briefly on the trail yesterday, but never exchanged names."

He turned back to me, holding out his hand, "I'm glad to see you again."

I shook his hand, "I'm glad to meet you for real, though, I don't know what to say." I turned to Rita who was watching this exchange with amusement. "It's actually a funny story, Miss Rita, but parts of it are kind of embarrassing."

"I can't wait to hear about it, but here, come into the living room and meet Emily. She sprained her ankle yesterday, so she's taking it easy on the couch today. Then you can tell us both the story."

"I think I met her yesterday also," I replied, following her into the next room.

Emily was lounging on the couch with her foot up on pillows and wrapped in ice packs. She smiled up at me as we were introduced, "I should have known it was going to be you when Aunt Rita was telling us about you and your happiness quest. I'm sorry I can't get up to say hello. As you see…" she motioned to her foot. "I swear it's broken, no matter what the doctor said."

She looked like an angel; her long dark hair was in soft waves against the pillows behind her. Tiny in comparison to her big brother. Her pixie-like features and wide smile reminded me of a young Halle Berry.

"You poor thing! How'd it happen?" I asked, my heart immediately going out to her.

"I was being a brat while Damien and I were wading in the river, so he came after me. I got my foot stuck between some rocks, though, it happened so fast that I really have no idea how I managed it. I was turning and trying to run in the water but wrenched it so badly that Damien had to rescue me instead." She looked fondly up at her brother, "and then he had to help me all the way back to the cars and bring me to the doctor. It definitely was not the way that I wanted to start off this trip."

"Oh my gosh, that sucks. How long are you here for?" I asked.

"It's just a long weekend, but it's looking like I'll end up being house-bound the whole time. It might not be what I had planned, but at least I'll get some quality time with Aunt Rita."

"I'm not complaining," Rita interjected, "You're a wonderful patient, and I love every minute I get to spend with you."

"A wonderful patient?" Damien pretended to be shocked, and everyone laughed. I could tell this family really loved each other, and I found I was relaxing in spite of myself.

"Sit down, Willa. Make yourself comfortable," Rita invited. "Can I get you something to drink?"

"No, but thank you. I'm okay right now," I replied, sitting down across from Emily on the other couch. Damien sat in a recliner to my right and grinned over at me.

"Okay, so what's the story? You all met on the trail yesterday?" Rita asked as she settled into the couch next to me.

Damien let out a loud laugh, and I felt my face get red again.

"Yes, sort of," I replied.

"Don't laugh, Damien!" Emily scolded her brother, "but, Willa, we do want to hear what prompted yesterday's shenanigans."

"Okay, I don't know how much your aunt has told you," I started to explain, "but summed up really quickly, I'm here on a little vacation. Sort of. I'm on what we've been calling a quest. I'm trying to figure out how to have happiness that comes from within and isn't based on people or circumstances. I want to have magical moments throughout my days, and feel like a Disney princess who could break out in song and dance at any moment."

I continued with a rush so I could get the embarrassing part out and have it over with, "I told my best friend that I would make her a video of myself singing and dancing in the woods, completely in costume. So, I went out on a trail yesterday in a fancy dress and I even made myself a flower crown. I heard clapping when I was finished, and there was Emily."

My face was flaming, and I put my hands on my cheeks to cool them down. "I only briefly met Damien as I walked back to the car, he didn't see my shenanigans."

"No, but Emily told me when I caught up to her at the swimming hole," he replied, grinning mischievously at me.

Rita was looking at us and smiling. "I can't imagine a better way for you to meet. You are pretty magical, Willa. I love that you did that, it sounds so fun."

"It actually was. But, after my interaction with Emily, I was so embarrassed that I didn't continue down the trail. I had planned on going swimming down at the end of the trail like you guys did. The reviews raved about that spot."

"Yeah, that's why we chose that trail too. The water was pretty cold though, we weren't in for long," Emily replied. "I think what you're doing is just awesome. More people should go searching for what they want in life and do silly things just because it's fun."

I nodded appreciatively at her. "Thank you."

Our dinner that evening was simple, but delicious, the conversation flowing easily. We talked about our lives, and hiking, and laughed together as Damien and Emily shared stories of their childhood. Most were stories of when they were visiting their aunt and uncle, and I could tell that it made Rita happy. Their obvious love for each other was such a beautiful thing to see.

When the evening was wrapping up, Emily turned to me. "You should go hiking with Damien tomorrow if you don't have plans already. I'm laid up on the couch and he's all alone, what if he breaks his foot and there's no one to save him?"

Damien glared at her, but then turned to me with a grin and said, "I was actually going to ask you the same thing. Would you want to?"

I laughed, "Sure. I have to check out of the house by eleven tomorrow morning, so I can meet you whenever."

"Just text me when you're ready. I know another good trail nearby that we can go down. It's not too long, I think it's around four miles, but there are some great views I think you'll love."

"Perfect," I pulled out my phone and handed it to him to put in his number.

"I want your number too," Rita said, hugging me.

"Of course," I replied, giving her a tight squeeze.

"Stay in touch. I want to know how this happiness quest of yours goes."

"Me too!" Emily said, "Don't leave me out. I may have a broken foot, but I want to be included."

We all laughed at that, and they passed around my phone adding their numbers.

My heart was so full when I left. To think I'd been so nervous about accepting Rita's invitation. This family was amazing.

The next morning, I sat and drank my coffee, relishing the quiet cool morning and beautiful surroundings. *One last time in this hammock porch swing. I have to figure out a time to bring Gina or my mom. They would love it here too.*

I wasn't in a hurry to leave, so I took out my notebook to add more. As I read over my previous entries, I realized that I hadn't asked Rita about her experiences with dealing with expectations. It just hadn't come up with the way the conversation went. *It's alright, I have her number, I'll just call her and talk about it at some point.*

Lost in contemplation, I started writing.

7. Don't be scared of strangers. They all have stories, and chances are, the stories will make your life better.

8. Family is important, but even more than blood family, taking people into your home and making them feel like family increases happiness on all sides. Genuine love makes such a difference.

It was time to get moving, Damien would be waiting for me if I didn't finish packing. As I did my final walk through, I added the rest of the Happy Mug Coffee to my food bag since the owners had said that I could take it. It was too good to leave behind. My phone vibrated with a text from Damien saying that he was on his way. He had also sent me directions to the trailhead where I was meeting him, so I regretfully got into my car and drove away from my perfect little cabin.

CHAPTER 11

There wasn't a whole lot of conversation when Damien and I began the trail. We were both feeling a little shy, I think. I know I was.

But, eventually I broke the silence with a question. "Would you mind if I asked your opinion on this whole happiness thing? I think it would be nice to hear some opinions from other people. I was going to bring it up last night but listening to you and your sister talk about your childhood seemed better."

"Did we overpower the conversation? I'm so sorry."

"It didn't really feel like that, I loved listening. I don't have much in the way of family, so listening to you all was special."

Damien flashed me a big smile. "Yeah, we love each other and laugh a lot. So, yes, ask me whatever you want."

"Okay, why do you think happiness is so elusive?" I asked.

"Ah. Good question. Well, I think there are a variety of reasons. The most common one is probably because we tend to live very selfishly. We are so concerned with our own lives, our own entertainment, that we forget how to live a life of purpose and service."

I felt myself do a slow blink. No one I knew talked like this.

"What does that even look like? A life of purpose and service..."

"It's different for everyone. We all have our talents, but more important-ly, we have our passions. I've found that if you're passionate about something, but the talent isn't there yet, putting in the work will get you to where you want to be. When you're doing the things you're passionate about, you'll find that everything falls into place."

"Do you have any real-life examples of what you mean?" My brain felt like it was being stretched. "I don't even really know if I know what I'm passionate about."

"Sure. My friend Diana, she's a perfect example. She felt like she was floundering through life. Just going through the motions, doing everything that society expects us to do, but she said she felt empty, bored, and unfulfilled.

She had a good job working for the state, but she told me that it never felt like it meant anything. Like literally anyone else could do her job if she wasn't there. Although, she did admit that maybe not everyone would have the same degree of success."

Damien paused as the trail crossed a creek. He jumped nimbly across. I followed, but less gracefully. The heel of my foot squished down into the mud.

"Oh shit!" My balance momentarily lost.

Damien grabbed my flailing arm and steadied me, laughing, "You just need longer legs."

"I'll go get some at Walmart when we get off this trail," I shot back, making a face at him. "Alright, continue," I requested, as we started up another incline. "What did Diana end up doing?"

"Well, Diana had always been passionate about art, but at this point had never taken the time to develop any talent of her own. So, one day she just decided to go for it. She started taking a bunch of different classes to figure out which medium she felt most inspired to create with."

"Oh gosh, I should do that," I interrupted. "That sounds amazing."

"I think so too," Damien agreed. "So anyway, spending time creating ended up really changing not only her mood but her outlook on life. She chose pottery as her medium and now, several years later, has art in galleries all over the country."

"That's so incredible. You don't often hear about artists that truly make it like that."

"I don't think it was really like that for her. In the beginning, she got involved in a city initiative that she knew about from her work that helped underprivileged kids. She was taking evening art classes at that point in addition to her regular job. She decided to spend her Saturdays volunteering with these kids, teaching them everything that she was learning. It was due to her work with the kids that she met gallery owners in the city, and they ended up trying out her pieces. But get this, they also feature art from at least one of her students alongside hers. She has since quit her job and works full-time as an artist and teacher. She says she's never felt more fulfilled and happier in her entire life."

"Wow. Just wow. That's such an awe-inspiring story."

We hiked in silence for a few minutes as I processed everything. "Does she live in Savannah also?" I asked.

"No, she's actually over in Raleigh. She moved there after college and I stayed in Georgia, but we've kept up with each other over the years. She inspires me to be better and do more myself."

"Can I ask? What does your life of purpose and service look like?"

"It's not nearly as inspiring as Diana's story," he replied, sounding a little embarrassed. "I told you last night, I'm a manager of a local grocery store. We pride ourselves on quality but cheap food. And, because I'm passionate about good food and feeding people, I'm a board member at our local food pantry and volunteer a lot of my free time. My store donates everything it can. At the pantry, instead of having people in need come pick it up, we deliver. It makes it a much more personalized service and we're able to actually connect with the people that we're feeding."

"Damien!" I exclaimed, "That's wonderful! And also very inspiring."

"Thanks. Sometimes I feel like I should be creating something like Diana does."

"But you are. You're creating relationships with people. If I had to bet, you don't just stop at feeding people, you help them in other ways, too. How many people that you've met through bringing them food have you hired at your grocery store?"

"Several," He responded, a little smile tugging at his lips.

"See, I knew it," I laughed. "You are making a difference in people's lives."

"Yes, you're right. And also, see how easy it was for me to slip into discontentment and away from happiness when I started comparing my life to Diana's?"

I nodded. "Happiness is a tricky little bugger, isn't it?"

"Very much so."

We got lost in our thoughts for a little while, trudging steadily up the mountain.

"Your aunt and I briefly talked about how expectations really mess up happiness also," I said, breaking the silence.

"Yeah, they definitely do."

"Do you have any advice on that?"

"I'm not an expert by any stretch of the imagination, because that's something I struggle with at times also. But I've actually been reading about a pseudo Danish philosophy called Jante. It basically says that no one is important."

"No one is important? What does that mean?" I asked.

"Well, the idea is that while I am an individual and therefore important in the most basic sense, it's the inflated ego of believing that I'm owed something that makes my expectations unrealistic."

"I don't think that I am owed anything," I replied, a little bit shocked by his response.

"I get that, Willa, but maybe think about it like this. People disappoint you because you expect them to behave, respond, or interact with you in a way that makes you feel respected or important. Maybe valued is a better way to put it."

"Are you saying that I shouldn't expect to be valued? That doesn't sound right."

"Not exactly. Imagine that you're standing on the beach at night, toes in the water. The great expanse of ocean in front of you and above you millions of stars reaching to the edge of the horizon. The feeling that you get in that moment, that you are a tiny, almost insignificant blip in the grand scheme of the universe. That feeling gives us a healthy perspective of our own importance, I think. If you can take that feeling, and then combine it with the idea that you alone are the one who is in control of your worth and happiness, then the opinions and actions of other people no longer weigh as heavily, either negatively or positively. Other people valuing you is nice, but unimportant, and on the flip side, people disrespecting you is unimportant also."

"That's an interesting way to look at it, for sure. I don't know how I feel about it, though. Part of it makes sense, but there is a part of me that rebels at the concept too."

Damien ducked under a low hanging branch and paused as I ducked under it also. "Yeah. It's not the way we were ever taught to think. I'm still working through it myself. I just don't want other people's opinions to end up defining my self-worth. Maybe it's a control thing, but when I read about that philosophy, I decided I would test it out in my own life and see what happens."

"But couldn't you also just take the good opinions that people have of you and use that for your self-worth? Especially if you choose the people that actually know you and love you?"

"Yes, you can, of course. I think that is a good practice, but I also think it's important to remember that there are times when it's easy to feel like the people nearest and dearest to you are biased, or don't see the whole of you. For instance, my sister loves me unconditionally, and we grew up together, so she knows me better than most. However, our lives are separate despite our closeness, so there are things that she just doesn't know. If I'm going through something that relates to things that she isn't as familiar with, I won't necessarily trust her opinion, even though she loves me. Or I won't trust her because I'll feel like her bias will complicate it, or I'll feel like she won't understand because of it."

"That's fair. But, just playing the devil's advocate here, you wouldn't trust your sister's opinion, but you'd trust the opinion of someone who didn't love you but knew more about the hypothetical situation? You'd allow the opinion of a stranger to define your self-worth in that instance?"

Damien laughed. "I'm not saying that it's right. I'm just saying that it happens. The way our brains work and the feelings that we have are just complicated and unreasonable sometimes."

"Well, you've given me plenty to think about for sure."

"Sorry about that." he replied ruefully. "It might not be the most thought-out response ever, because it's still something that I'm working through."

"No!" I exclaimed, "It was good. I'd never even considered it from that direction before, so I appreciate your point of view."

He smiled back at me, "Okay, good."

CHAPTER 12

I texted Christy when I left Damien that afternoon.

"So, I met this guy that thinks that happiness comes from living a life of purpose and service. What do you think about that? He said that people think too highly of themselves and that people need to realize their place in the universe to help manage expectations. He also said in relation to that, that we shouldn't expect people to treat us with respect which just sounded wrong to me. There was something about comparison also, but we didn't talk too much about that, it kind of seems obvious, so I'll add that to my notebook."

I waited a few minutes to see if she'd respond, and when she didn't, I put the car in reverse and headed out. *She must be busy.*

My plan was to drive up to the Cherokee Indian Reservation and check out that area. Rita had suggested it last night, and when I had googled it, it looked like there would be a lot of interesting things to see. People had even mentioned that they had seen Elk eating by the sides of the road up there. That would be pretty incredible, so I was excited for this next stage of my trip.

I found myself driving along without the radio on. There was too much to look at and so much to think about.

Damien's story was such an inspiring one as was the story of his friend. I wanted so badly to be able to have a story like that, one that could be told and other people were better for having heard it. *This adventure is the most interesting and inspiring thing that has ever happened to me, but who will I be at the end of it? Will I actually be able to live a life that is a happily ever after? But what was my life of purpose and service? What am I passionate about?* I didn't have an answer for that, so I decided just to relax and enjoy the scenery of this drive.

The day had gotten cloudy by the time I got off the Blue Ridge Parkway in Cherokee. There was an old grist mill to the right that promised historic significance and a few trails. Or, if I turned left, I'd go straight into town. I decided that I wasn't ready to go to town, so I turned right and went to find Mingus Mill. The ancient building was off to my left as I got out of my car, but I decided to check that out on my way back. I threw my umbrella in my little bag, just in case the clouds decided to release, and headed down the trail by the creek. I was finding that there was such a serenity found on the trails that followed the water. Even with the clouds, this was a beautiful day. I sat down under a tree after walking for a while and pulled out my happiness notebook.

9. Walking beside this creek is a revelation in the sense of the harmony in movement. It made me realize that the movement of the water and the movement of my body gives me the sense that time had slowed to the rhythm of my steps. It feels like for once I am not being left behind, but moving along with it. I'm not rushing to catch up or slowing down. I'm simply existing at the same time and flow as the world around me. I've never considered anything like this before, it's such a weird feeling. I wonder if the artificial rhythms of city life are a contributing factor to feeling off and discontent. Because this, this just makes me feel in line with the universe. I guess this is what my mom and Christy were talking about. It makes me wonder why anyone lives in the city. This is so much better.

A raindrop plopped down with a giant splat on my notebook. I wiped it off, trying to not smudge the ink, and closed the notebook, tucking it back into my pack. I pulled out my umbrella as the rain started coming down in earnest. Even with the umbrella I was getting drenched. I kicked at a puddle and laughed. My mom and I had recently watched Singing in the Rain together. It had been one of our favorites when I was growing up. She was going to love that this had happened. I began humming the title song from the movie, twirling my umbrella and pretending the trees were the lampposts. As I was finishing the song, and dancing with a tree, I heard a voice. "May I have this dance?"

Startled, I spun around. A man, a really good looking man, was standing there smiling at me, his hand outstretched. Without even thinking, I put my hand in his. He continued humming the song and we danced, splashing and laughing. At the end of the song, he tucked my hand under his arm, and we walked back towards the parking lot.

"That was probably the craziest thing I've ever done," he said with a chuckle, "but, I couldn't resist. The trees couldn't get all the action. My name is Ethan Musgraves," he added, smiling at me. He had the most beautiful blue eyes and curling blonde lashes I'd ever seen.

"Willa Cameron," I replied. "Thank you for the dance. That was the most fun I've had in a long time."

He was probably my age, a little bit taller than me, a dusky shadow of a beard on his face contrasted with the blonde of his short faded hair. It was obvious that he spent his time in a professional setting with a haircut like that. *Of course I notice his haircut. God, I've been in the salon business too long.*

We were both drenched to the skin, and I was sure that I looked a fright. *Obviously, I would meet the most handsome man I've ever seen in my life when I'm behaving like a crazy person in the rain.* I sighed inwardly.

He looked over at me, "I'm so glad to meet you, Willa Cameron. Are you, by any chance, a water sprite and not a human at all?"

I laughed. "I feel more like a water rat at this point, and I'm sure I look like one too."

"Not at all. I have your hand because I was afraid that if I let go, you'd disappear." His grin made my heart stop.

"I'm not going anywhere," I replied, smiling back at him.

"Forgive me if I just hold on a little longer while I struggle to believe you," He winked at me. "I know I'm being silly; I just feel like I've stepped into an old movie."

I giggled, "I know what you mean."

The rain ended just as quickly as it had begun as we continued our trudge back down the trail. I had a feeling we'd get back to the cars much too quickly. The sudden downpour had filled the creek and it had risen above its banks. As we approached the mill, we could see the excess water being released in a cascading waterfall from the flume.

"It's really an incredible feat of engineering, isn't it?" I said, marveling at the structure that still worked more than a hundred years after it had been built.

"Yes, it really is. Did you go look at it when you got here?"

"Not really," I replied. "Obviously I saw it when I walked past it on this side, but I didn't go over there."

"Let's go look at it then."

"Okay," I agreed, "but did you go look at it already?"

"Yes, but it's so awesome, and I'd like to see it with you."

"Would you?" I asked, a teasing grin on my face.

"Yes, I would," he replied, squeezing my arm that was still tucked in his. It was surprising how comfortable it was to walk with him like this. We reached the cars, and he paused next to a gray Subaru. "Hey, I wanna throw my pack in the car, if you don't mind, and then we can walk over."

"Of course, that's a good idea," I agreed, I didn't want to be carrying my little bag anymore either.

He let go of my arm and I brushed my drenched hair away from my face.

"Honestly," I said, hesitantly, "I'd really like to change into something dry before we go see the mill. I have a change of clothes in the car. It's just with this breeze I'm freezing now." There were goosebumps on my arms. It wasn't that cold out, but being soaked combined with the wind was killing me.

"No, that's a great idea. I'll do that too."

My car was only three spaces away from his. I dropped my dripping wet bag on the floor of the car, taking my notebook out so that it wouldn't sit in the damp.

"You're from Florida also?" he asked, as he approached holding a roll of dry clothes and a towel. "I noticed your license plate."

"Yeah, I'm in Orlando, how about you?" I asked, closing the door of the car. I had my overnight bag in my hand.

"Clearwater Beach."

"Nice! That's not too far when you don't hit traffic." We walked together towards the public bathrooms. "What do you do for work?" I asked.

"I teach literature at the University of South Florida. How about you?"

"Oh wow! I do hair, so I have a booth in a salon in Winter Park."

"That's a good skill to have. It's definitely an art form."

"Thanks. I appreciate you saying that," I replied, gratefully. "Sometimes it feels like it's not a very useful job, in the grand scheme of things anyway. I mean, how am I making the world a better place?" I blushed. "That sounds way more intense than I meant it to."

We had stopped where the sidewalk branched to take us in different directions.

"Really? I want to answer that, but let's go change first because I don't want you to be cold."

I smiled at him gratefully. "Okay."

I walked into the bathroom, my mind racing. *Who was this guy? How does someone so thoughtful exist? Dancing in the rain with a complete stranger, who happens to actually live two hours away from me, but we meet hundreds of miles away? I hope he doesn't think I'm too intense after that "make the world a better place" comment.* Catching sight of myself in the mirror, I stopped, horrified. I did look like a water rat. My hair was matted down, my eye makeup had run a little bit, and there were definite racoon eyes happening. *Not even close to a water sprite, sir. You were way too kind.*

I went into the stall and stripped out of my drenched t-shirt and shorts. When I was done drying off, I pulled out a long blue flowing skirt and a white tank top. It might not be exactly hiking clothes, but I needed him to see that I could be presentable. I dried my hair as best I could with the towel and shook it out. The mirror over the sinks wasn't the best, but I fixed my makeup quickly knowing that Ethan would be waiting on me.

I walked back outside, my wet clothes and towel bundled in one hand, and my bag in the other. Ethan was waiting at the point the sidewalk diverged, still holding his wet clothes also. My breath caught. He had changed into a t-shirt and jeans that fit him very well. He was very attractive.

"You are a water sprite. I knew it," he said smiling, as I walked up to him.

I blushed. "The mirror definitely said otherwise when I walked into the bathroom, sir."

"You sell yourself short," he replied, his gaze still admiring.

"I appreciate it," I smiled back. I never knew what to do with compliments, they tended to make me feel even more awkward, but it was nice that he liked what he saw.

We walked to the cars, deposited our bundles, and headed back towards the mill.

"May I?" Ethan asked, reaching for my arm and placing it in his.

"Of course," I smiled at him. He was so different from anyone that I had ever met. It didn't seem possible that we were strangers, it just felt so natural.

"So, back to what we were talking about before," he said, and then paused, "You look incredible, by the way, in case I didn't mention that before."

I blushed again. "Thanks, you too."

He smiled appreciatively, "So, anyway, I was going to say earlier, I think a hair stylist makes the world better by helping people feel good about themselves. I think most people find a lot of their self-worth in how they look. It shouldn't be that way, but I think it is."

"I've never thought about it like that." I replied, thoughtfully, "Thank you for saying that. It is definitely one of the best parts about my job, watching them when they look in the mirror and start to glow. Another happiness thing to add to my notebook."

"Happiness thing?" Ethan looked at me quizzically.

"Yes, I'm on a quest," I grinned mischievously. "A happiness quest according to my mom."

"This is intriguing! Tell me more."

We were approaching the mill at this point and could see an old man sitting in a chair just on the other side of the window. There was movement, and then the sounds of a banjo reached us.

"Of course I'll tell you, but oh my god! Where have you brought me?" I laughed, totally distracted.

"Apparently we've been transported to West Virginia." He was laughing too. "I swear when I was over here earlier there was no old man playing a banjo, but I have to say, this is kind of amazing."

"My adventure would not have been complete without this." I grinned over at him, "I didn't even know what I was missing."

He winked at me. We paused for a moment outside the door to the mill, listening to the banjo.

"Tell me about this happiness quest of yours," Ethan repeated, as we continued past the mill and up the path next to the flume.

"Well, it started with a conversation I had with my mom. I've been feeling like I'm just going through the motions of life, and I want more. I told her that I just want to feel like I can break out into song at any point like the Disney princesses do because there's a sense of joy deep inside of me. She suggested that I would be able to figure it out if I came to the woods because life is simpler out here. I didn't know what she meant then, but I feel like I'm starting to understand now."

Ethan was nodding in agreement, so I continued. "This is my fourth day exploring, I've met some absolutely incredible people so far who have given me so much to think about. I started writing down all the things I've been learning because I didn't want to forget anything, so that's the happiness notebook I mentioned. I want to keep talking to people and hearing about what happiness means to them and where they find it." I paused, suddenly self-conscious, "Do I sound like a crazy person? Sometimes I think so."

"No, not at all!" he exclaimed, "I think it's wonderful that you're doing this."

"Thank you." It felt really good to hear him say that. We had walked to the end of the flume and were standing at the spot where the creek was diverted. "This is just amazing. Thank you for bringing me up here."

"You're welcome. I hoped that you would think it was as cool as I did."

"I do, for sure," I affirmed, awed by the wooden infrastructure and ancient engineering. "So, what's your story, Ethan? What brings you up this way?"

"I'm on summer sabbatical from work. My parents live in Charlotte, so I went to visit them this past week. I'm headed over to Wesser right now, I'm actually starting a hiking trip tomorrow on the Appalachian trail going from Wesser up to Pearisburg in Virginia. It'll take me about a month."

"Oh! I was going to go to Wesser, too. What made you stop here, though, this is not really on the way, is it?" I asked.

"No, not really, but it's not too bad of a detour. I wanted to take the Blue Ridge Parkway across and then go down. It's just so much better than the regular highway."

"Oh, I agree. I took it up here from where I was down near Saluda. It was my first time on it and those views are just incredible."

Ethan nodded and continued, "I was tired of driving when I got off the parkway and I saw that this was a point of interest on the map, so I stopped to explore. Do you want to see inside the mill?" he asked as we approached the building again.

The old man was no longer playing the banjo, but was standing at the door and reaching to shut it.

"Oh, what time is it? They must be closing."

"It's 5 o'clock already," I replied, looking at my watch, shocked. This day had gone by so fast.

"Well, would you be interested in getting dinner with me in town?" Ethan asked. "I would like to spend more time with you."

"I would love to," I replied simply. Already it felt like we had so much in common, just in our appreciation of nature, human ingenuity, classic movies, and romantic gestures. I found myself wanting to know everything I possibly could about this man.

"Good," he said, smiling at me, "The place I'm staying at in Wesser should only be like 30 minutes from here. I want to get an early morning start on the trail tomorrow, but we have this evening to hang out, if you don't have plans already?"

"No, no plans yet. My friend in Saluda just told me to check out this area, so that's why I'm here."

We settled on a Mexican restaurant on the other end of town. My head was spinning on the drive over there. Ethan was tall and fit, his face chiseled. His smile, a little bit crooked, was like sunshine. *No no no, Willa! I told myself. This trip was supposed to not have any boys.* I couldn't believe that he had actually danced with me in the rain, who does that with a perfect stranger? *How could he possibly be single, he was single, wasn't he?* I took a deep breath before I got out of the car. *Let's just see where this goes.* I told myself firmly. He is a little bit of magic to add to this adventure. Just breathe and see what happens.

Ethan was waiting for me behind my car. "Can I hold your hand?" he asked, as I joined him.

I slipped my hand into his. "Yes," I smiled at him. I thought it was adorable that he wanted to. My dad had told me once a long time ago that I'd know when I held his hand if it was meant to be. A sudden thought came to me. *I had never held Peter's hand like this. There had always been that weird thing of not wanting to cross any boundaries. No. No thinking about Peter, this doesn't concern him.*

"What are you thinking about?" Ethan asked, startling me out of my thoughts.

"I was thinking how comfortable it is to hold your hand," I replied, it was not the time to tell him all of the thoughts. "Do you dance with strangers in the rain very often?"

He laughed as he opened the door to the restaurant for me, "No, you're definitely the first."

We sat down at the table the host brought us to and opened our menus. Conversation came easily. I told him about the cabin I'd stayed in, meeting Rita and Evie and then Rita's family. He laughed when I told him about dancing in the princess dress and Emily catching me. "So, you do make a habit of dancing in the woods! You are a fairy creature!"

"No! I mean, twice doesn't make it a habit, but I'm definitely down for becoming a fairy creature." I giggled, "Alright, though, enough about me. Tell me more about your trip. You said it's going to take you a month?"

"Yes. I actually hiked the whole thing in my early twenties, but I really loved this stretch, so I'm doing it again."

"You hiked the whole Appalachian trail?" I asked, impressed.

"Yeah, it was life changing. After I got into teaching, I've still tried to do a big hike every summer."

"You said your parents live up here, are you from here, or are you from Florida?"

"I'm from here. I moved to Florida 6 years ago with my ex fiancée. She left me the day before we got married about 3 years ago. By that point I was really enjoying my job at the university, so I stayed. There's so much to explore in central Florida, I haven't gotten bored yet."

"She left you the day before your wedding?" I exclaimed, shocked.

"Yeah, she didn't even talk to me for more than a year afterwards. She'd been cheating on me for a while, I guess. The day before the wedding she sent me an email while I was finishing up some last minute things at work. She said that she couldn't go through with it. Told me about the affairs and said that she'd have her things out of our apartment by the time I got home. She said not to contact her further. I was devastated. I haven't done much dating since, to be honest."

"I understand that for sure. That's horrible, I'm so sorry she did that to you." My heart hurt for him. "I haven't done a whole lot of dating the past few years either, but not for any good reason. I've just been hanging out with my friends. I thought something might develop with my friend Peter, but it never did, and he is very much in love with his girlfriend now." I felt like if he was going to be so upfront about his ex, I should tell him at least that Peter existed.

CHAPTER 13

"Would you mind if I texted you during my hike?" Ethan asked, after giving me his phone number. We were standing in the parking lot, dinner was done, but neither one of us were ready to leave.

"Of course not. I would love to hear how it's going."

"I'm going to want to hear about the rest of this 'happiness quest' of yours too. I don't think you told me yet, how long are you going to be up here?"

"It's pretty flexible, I opened up my schedule for a little over a week, but I wasn't sure if it was going to be done in 2 weeks or 2 days. I can adjust as needed."

"Oh. Gotcha," he paused for a moment. "Well, I should probably get going."

I was not ready to leave him, but I couldn't think of any other excuses to continue the conversation. Besides, I knew he still had to drive to Wesser and I needed to figure out where I was going to stay tonight. I had wanted to do a hike on the Appalachian trail, but I didn't want him to think that I was following him. So, I smiled, "Yeah, thank you again for dinner. This has been an amazing evening."

"Yes, yes it has," Ethan agreed. "I'm so glad to have met you, Willa. Can I text you later after I get to my hotel?"

My heart stopped again, this man knew all the ways to my heart. "Yes, please."

"Okay, good." We were smiling at each other, and I could tell he wanted to kiss me, but he turned away. "I'll text you in a little while."

We got into our cars. He really did seem wonderful and interesting, but I tried to temper my excitement. I wasn't supposed to be finding happiness by finding a man.

I texted Gina, "I have so much to tell you. Want it now or when I come back?"

I looked up places to stay while I waited for her response.

"Of course I want it now, but I'm out with Tommy and Peter right now. So, maybe just wait? Do you know when you're coming home?" she responded a few minutes later.

"No, I'm not sure yet. Alright. I'll save it all for when I get back. Love you."

"I love you too. Be careful."

I had gotten a text from Christy, "I have a full evening, but I promise I'll respond first thing in the morning. I love your questions and the things you're talking about."

"No worries." I responded. "Talk to you tomorrow, have a good night."

I closed out the messages and looked up places to stay in the area. I found that the KOA had a cabin that was way cheaper than spending the night in a hotel, so I booked it. It was only a short drive away through the Cherokee reservation, located on the banks of a small river.

I bought firewood when I checked in and, after depositing my belongings on the bed in the cabin, I set about building a fire. The rain earlier had cooled everything down, so it was a little bit chilly and the perfect temperature for sitting by the fire pit.

I settled down in one of the chairs with my Happiness notebook and began writing.

10. I met someone today who reminded me of a bit of happiness from my regular life. The look on people's faces when I finish their hair and they know they look even better than before.

11. On that same line of thinking, being reminded (either by yourself or by someone else) of things that you do well is important also.

12. Dance in the rain. I drew a winking face and a heart. I wasn't ready to write any more about it yet, so that would have to do for now.

My phone vibrated and my heart leaped into my throat when I saw his name. Ethan.

"Hey! Did you find a place to stay tonight?"

"Yeah, a cabin at the KOA. I've got a fire and my notebook, it's pretty awesome."

"Sounds like it. Wish I was there too."

"That would make it perfect." I typed and then erased. *That's coming on way too strong, Willa. Chill.*

I settled on just a short "Yeah!" followed by an immediate question, "So, I thought of this after we left, is your car just going to stay there for your whole trip?"

"No, I have some friends that live in Asheville. They're going to come out and get it. They'll bring it up to me in Pearisburg when I'm finished."

"Oh, wow! That's nice of them!"

"Yeah, I've known Chris my whole life. He and his wife lead a ministry for abused kids."

I clicked on the heart eyes emoji, then added "That's amazing."

All of these people I keep meeting or hearing about, how do I not know any of these people where I live? It can't be that all these incredible lives are lived somewhere else besides Central Florida, but why don't I know any?

A few minutes passed, I was wracking my brain trying to come up with something else to say, but I didn't know what. Everything that I thought of just sounded so pathetic.

"Willa, I'm falling asleep. I'll talk to you tomorrow?"

"Yes of course! Sleep well."

"I will. I'm so glad to have met you."

My smile would not be contained, "I'm so glad to have met you too. Good night!"

I put down my phone and stared into the fire, blissfully happy.

Going back to my notebook, I began writing again.

At this moment I am so happy. I am grateful for so many things, for my mom suggesting this trip, for everyone I've met up here so far, for the beautiful weather, and most of all, the absolutely magical moments. And Ethan.

I closed the notebook and stared into the fire as I let it burn out for the night. My hair smelled deliciously of the campfire when I curled up in the bed a little while later, and sleep came quickly.

My phone vibrated, startling me awake what felt like a few moments later. The sun shining through the window though, said otherwise.

"Meet me at Stecoah?" I smiled. It was Ethan. *What's Stecoah?* I googled it. It was a little town not too far away, the Appalachian trail crossed the road not far from it.

"Good morning! Yes!!" I responded.

"I was thinking if you wanted to, we could hike together up to Fontana Dam and maybe spend a little time there before I have to get back on the trail."

"That sounds awesome. I'd love that."

Oh my God, what am I doing? I'm going to go hiking with a stranger, a really good looking one who gives me butterflies. This might be one of my more insane decisions. My mom would probably give me shit when she found out.

Another text came in, "I am going to spend the night at the shelter not too far from there. But I'll meet you at the crossroads tomorrow, probably by like ten, if that sounds good to you."

"Yes!"

"Can I call you?"

I didn't respond, just hit the call button.

"Hey!" Ethan answered, "Good morning."

"Good morning."

"I just woke up thinking about you," he said, making my heart beat faster, "and I just thought if you were going hiking in the area, you might be up for joining me for a short stretch."

My smile could not be contained as I answered him, "Yes! I was wanting to do a hike on the Appalachian Trail, but hadn't settled on which part to do. This will be perfect. And doing it with you will be even better."

"Okay good," I could hear the smile in his voice as well.

"Is there parking there at the Stecoah trailhead?"

"Yes, but you may want to park at Fontana and get a ride down to Stecoah. That way you won't have to hike back to your car. They have a few drivers that go out to Fontana to help hikers get into town," he responded.

"Oh yeah, that's a good idea. So, I've never actually done an overnight hike, do I need to bring anything specific?"

"We'll be at Fontana that night. You said you brought some things to camp with, right?"

"Yeah, I brought a hammock and a sleeping bag."

"That works. You can share my tent if you want, instead of sleeping in a hammock. I like hammocks for naps, but not all night. I need to stretch out."

We laughed and he added, "You'll just need to bring something to eat on the trail. And some water."

"I can do that. Yay! I'm so excited!"

"Yeah, me too," he agreed, "Alright, I'll talk to you later."

"Okay. See you tomorrow." I felt like a giddy teenager as I hung up the phone. There was no way that I was going to go back to sleep now. I was way too excited. *I don't even know what is happening.* I felt like I could run for miles and running was not even something I did regularly. I giggled at that thought. *Today is off to the best start.*

CHAPTER 14

There wasn't really anything on my list of things to do for the day, so I decided to go check out Stecoah and Fontana Dam in preparation for tomorrow. I like surprises, but even more, I like knowing what I'm getting myself into, especially when in the company of a cute guy. Besides, I needed to see if I could get shuttled from where I'd leave my car at Fontana Dam down to the Stecoah trail head.

I was just finishing up my check out process when Christy texted.

"Good morning! I hope you slept well!"

"Yes!" I replied, "Good morning! I didn't mean to bother you yesterday when you were busy."

"It's no problem, I just didn't have the time to give your questions the amount of time they deserved. So anyway, these are my thoughts:

1: A life of service and purpose, I totally agree with him on that. The more we are satisfied with ourselves, the happier we are. That satisfaction is usually found when we find our passion and do it, and it's also found when we are helping people, or animals, or even the planet.

2: As far as people thinking too highly of themselves and needing to realize their place in the universe, I can't discount that either. It's human nature, probably bred from our society, to be concerned with only what involves us, or touches our lives. Everything is connected and, sadly to say, the world doesn't revolve around either one of us. It might be easier if it did." She inserted a laughing emoji.

I replied with a few laughing faces, and she continued,

"3: I'm not entirely sure what the guy meant about respect, because everyone and everything is deserving of respect, whether you align or not. But with it being in relation to our place in the world and managing expectations, maybe he just meant that we tend to place too much emphasis on our identity and what we deserve rather than realizing that there is always a bigger picture and that we don't know everything."

"That's fair," I responded. "It's definitely a lot to think about. I'm leaving to go out on my next adventure. I'll text you in a couple days to tell you about it."

"Sounds good. Have so much fun!"

I headed out. The anticipation made the drive feel long, and the switchbacks up the mountain made me grateful that I was the driver and not a passenger. Had it been otherwise I was certain I would be feeling nauseous. But the view from the top of the mountain looking down at Fontana Dam and the lake it had created was well worth it all. The bright blue sky, the new greens of spring, the puffy white clouds and the sun shining off the water, I sighed. *How could a place be this perfect?* A woman came up the path beside me and stood nearby gazing out over the overlook with me.

"It's really incredible, isn't it?" I asked.

"Yes. And it's such a beautiful day, even though these mornings are a bit chilly."

"Are you a thru hiker?" She wasn't wearing a pack, but her clothes seemed to suggest that she might be.

"Yes, my group and I are having a rest day here and catching up on laundry. Are you hiking?"

"No, I mean, sort of. I've just been doing a few short hikes in the area. But I'm actually meeting a new friend of mine down at Stecoah tomorrow and joining him for the hike up here. He's going up to somewhere in Virginia. But I think hiking the whole trail would be incredible. It's so cool that you're doing it."

"Yeah. My friends and I really love this hike, especially this area," she replied, "If you want, you can come down to our camp and meet them. We love talking about the trail and our experiences."

"That would be awesome. I'd love to hear your stories."

"Well, come on then," she replied, turning away. She headed down the stairs that led to the camping area, and I quickly followed.

"My name is Bethany, by the way," she added, smiling back at me.

"I'm Willa. It's nice to meet you."

As we got to the bottom of the steps, Bethany gestured widely, "Welcome to the Fontana Hilton!"

I didn't know what to expect, but I was intrigued by the cabin-like exterior. As we rounded the building, though, I found out that it was not a cabin at all, but merely a shelter with bunks on the right and left for campers to sleep on hardwood up off the floor.

"We use the shelters mostly just to get out of the rain, but this one is the nicest, or at least one of the nicest, on the trail. Most of us like sleeping in our tents, though, unless there is bad weather. Here, meet the gang."

Four others sat around a fire pit in the gravel yard. A few picnic tables, a water spicket, and a solar charging station scattered the yard also.

"This is Willa, everyone. She's a newbie to the trail and wants to hear stories," Bethany said, introducing me. "Willa, this is Annalisa, Noelle, Derek, and Mark. We've all been friends since college. We try to take a hiking trip together every couple of years, so here we are. We are trying to do the whole trail, but, depending on time, all of us might not make it the entire way."

"Hey, Willa!" The friendliness and obvious welcome on their faces felt a little surprising.

City life has really made me introverted. Why was talking to strangers intimidating? I made a mental note to write about that in my happiness notebook.

I smiled at them. This was a group, probably a few years older than I, that gave off the vibe of calm experience. "Hi everyone!"

"Here, Willa, sit. Where are you from, what brings you to the trail?" Mark said, kindly, motioning to a spot on one of the benches near the fire.

"I'm from the Orlando area, and I'm here because I'm on a quest for happiness." I grinned. I still had a hard time saying that with a straight face.

They chuckled, "Tell us more," Derek encouraged.

"Well, I know it's crazy, but there's been so many times during my life lately that I just feel like I'm going through the motions. It's not that I'm sad or depressed, necessarily, I'm just sort of meh feeling. I don't really know how to explain it better than that."

I noticed that a few of them were nodding in agreement, so I continued, "I was talking to my mom the other day about how I just want a happily ever after, and not the Disney Princess version, I just want to live happily for the rest of my life. But I don't know how. Anyway, she suggested that I come out here to the woods to try to figure it out. So here I am."

"That is amazing," Derek responded first. "I think we can all relate."

"For sure," Bethany agreed. "That's something I've been focused on for some time now."

"Really?" I asked, my surprise evident.

"Yeah, actually. I have some theories on it, if you want to hear them."

"I really do. But I don't know if everyone here wants to talk about this now? I know I kind of got deep really quickly."

The others were all nodding encouragingly, though, "I think this is probably one of the best conversation topics we could have today," Annalisa said.

"You'll find that we're a pretty self-aware group, and we all really love talking about things that really matter and help us be better people," Mark added. "So, yes, by all means, Beth, share what you've learned."

"Alright," Bethany began, "I really believe that when you get down to the very base of the issue that you'll find that being comfortable with who you are and knowing that you are loved and loveable is the key to happiness."

"Oh yeah!" Noelle agreed quickly.

"That does make sense." I replied, "But I don't think that's as easy as it sounds."

"No, of course not." Bethany said. "I have noticed that so many people have a false narrative running through their heads telling them that they are a screw up."

Mark raised his hand. "Me. For sure."

We all looked over at him. "Aw, come on guys. I can't be the only one."

"You're not," Bethany responded.

We all nodded in agreement.

She continued, "I think everyone struggles with this to some degree, whether we're focused on that thing we did on Tuesday that everyone is surely judging us for, or that moment last year that we didn't choose to do the right thing. I think everyone has their own things that trip them up."

"How do you beat the false narrative?" I asked.

"I've found that it's a constant battle," she responded. "It gets easier with time, but it's something that you always have to be aware of. It seems to attack at just the right moment when you're at your weakest."

"What do you do to fight it, though?"

"Well, first of all, I think you have to realize that it's your mind that's bringing you to a dark place. At first, even that is difficult. But when you start feeling the more negative emotions taking over, take a moment to realize your thoughts. Are you truly upset about something that happened or is your mind saying things that aren't realistic or true? Basically you're rewiring your brain to have healthy responses, instead of the automatic negativity that comes so easily."

"When you say it like that it doesn't sound that difficult," Derek objected.

"Oh no," Bethany replied, "it's very hard. The process might be simplistic in concept, but in practice you really have to basically go to war with your brain to force it into new patterns. Some people find it easier than others, but it's definitely a challenge, especially at first. We tend to let our brains control us instead of it being the other way around."

Derek put up his hand, "Wait a second, at that point you'd be using your brain to control your brain. I feel like this is a messy theory."

We all laughed.

"I'm not an expert," Bethany protested good naturedly. "I've done some reading about it, but mostly just talked to people trying to discover what their self-talk is like and what they do about it. It's really fascinating, everyone's a little bit different, and no one really talks about it because we're afraid that people will think that we're crazy or because they think that everyone has the same thing."

"I don't think I have an inner monologue," Annalisa interjected.

"Wait, what?" Noelle asked, as all of us looked at Annalisa in surprise.

"Is an inner monologue the same as self-talk?" I asked, feeling a little bit confused. No one I knew talked about anything like this.

"Yes," Annalisa responded, "It came up before with my friends, and that's what we called it. It was actually because there was some meme going around on social media that brought it up. Some people, like myself, don't really have a voice or thought patterns that really talk to myself."

"I didn't know that was a thing," Bethany said. "Everyone I've ever talked to about it has had some variation."

"It's kind of hard to explain, but, for me, I imagine scenarios in the future and occasionally revisit scenes from the past. I think about things that I'm doing or processing through in the present, but there's never something directed at myself."

"Wow! I am so jealous," Mark replied, "Here I am having to tell my brain to shut up, just so that I can talk right now, and it's like 'Why are you telling them this? They'll think you're crazy!' Yet, here I am. That's progress, right, Beth?"

"Very much so."

There was a lull in conversation, so I asked Bethany, "You said at the beginning that it has something to do with love and being comfortable with yourself."

"Yes, I've noticed in my own life that I struggle with loving myself. It's not an easy thing to admit to, honestly. But I find that a lot of the time I can be very critical of myself, often feeling like I'm not good enough. Sometimes it seems like everyone is better at life than I am. They're more attractive, better at relationships, funnier, smarter, in better shape, just everything. It feels like I have to fight so hard to get anywhere, that there's this despair that just creeps up and latches hold of me. From that despair the false narrative begins shouting at me." She paused, gathering her thoughts.

Annalisa spoke up, "Bethany, I had no idea..." her voice trailing off, and we could see tears glistening in her eyes.

"It's okay, Annalisa, not something I want to acknowledge often, but it's important to the point I'm trying to make. Willa, it's when I stop and remember that I have people in my life who truly do love me, and make myself start naming positive things about myself, that I can get the false narrative to shut up. I also think it's good to remind myself that my worth is not based on superficial things. Integrity is one of the biggest contributors to self-worth. If your actions match your words, and you're putting in your best effort in all that you do, you'll find it so much easier to silence any negativity from yourself or even other people."

We were all silent for a few minutes, just watching the fire and thinking about Bethany's words.

"Okay. So, the next question," I asked the group, "Where do you find you're happiest?"

"On the trail," Noelle answered immediately, and we all laughed.

"Yeah, I think that's all of our answers, "Derek agreed.

"I should have guessed that," my face flaming with self-consciousness, "I guess I should have asked it this way, where do you find your happiness when you're home?"

"I would like to share some thoughts on this, if the rest of you don't mind," Mark's tone was apologetic, and I realized that I understood why his tone was self-effacing since he had just explained what his inner monologue was like. *Maybe understanding people and having compassion for them would be so much easier if everyone knew what the other's inner voice was like...* the thought trailed away as Bethany answered him.

"Please do, Mark."

"Well," he began, "I once read something that said that happiness is not getting or having everything that you want. True happiness lies in being content and not craving more, and truly just being at peace. It really hit me hard because I think society teaches us to always want more. 'The grass is always greener on the other side, so keep chasing it. Enough is never enough.' So, for me, finding that inner peace, finding the things that make me peaceful in my daily life, has been crucial to figuring out how to have a happy life."

"Oh yes!" Derek exclaimed, "I agree. Being content is a seriously under-rated virtue."

I nodded in agreement and turned back to Mark, "What are the things that you do to make yourself peaceful and content, though?"

He thought for a moment. "I think if I was bringing it down to the very basics, it looks like gratitude. Gratitude for what I have, but also for the opportunities that I've been given and for the people in my life. Everything changes, but, while that can be difficult and stressful, I can usually find my way if I'm actively noticing the things that I am thankful for."

I smiled, delighted with his response. "I had a conversation with two older women in Saluda a few days ago who also agreed with you. Gratitude was their key to happiness also, but I guess I never really tied gratitude with being content and at peace, though."

I paused, "I guess my next question might be a little invasive, but what does your life look like, Mark? I get the concept, but in practice, what does it look like for you?"

"Well, I'm an electrician by trade, so I see ups and downs in business on a regular basis. I'm recently divorced, but with no kids, and I've had to come to terms with my ex's decision to leave our marriage. And then of course there's the things that happen on a daily basis that seem to conspire to throw off the balance of peace. My way of maintaining that balance is to remind myself of all the things that I am thankful for when everything gets too overwhelming. I also make it a practice to get out on a trail somewhere around where I live at least once a week."

"Oooh, wow!"

"Yeah, our Mark has been through the wringer lately," Annalisa said, patting Mark's arm. "I think we all needed this trip."

CHAPTER 15

I drove back down the mountain a few hours later. The conversation with Bethany, Derck, Annalisa, Noelle, and Mark had continued well into the afternoon. They had shared their stories of how they met in college, and how they had gone their separate ways afterwards. But their love of nature and hiking had kept them together, doing one long hike every two or three years.

They all had shared their methods for finding happiness in their daily lives. There were common themes of spending as much time outdoors, being as physically active as possible, and helping people in some way.

Annalisa was a kindergarten teacher, and everything about her showed how much she cared about everyone. But she was unable to have her own children and felt that pain keenly. She said that her happiness was found in her job and spreading as much love as she could to all who needed it. She stayed active doing Ninja Warrior workouts.

Bethany ran a small boutique consignment shop and taught yoga on the side. She said that her happiness was found when she was cognizant of her thoughts and feelings and used movement to keep herself in the present. She said that it was important to her to be certain that her actions had the integrity of being faithful to what she believed to be true and right. She had added that she found that sustainable fashion was a way that she could make a living and help the environment at the same time, and teaching yoga was a way for her to stay mindful and help others.

Derek had expounded on his life as one who had been a jack of all trades. He was currently a martial arts instructor at a gym and loved it. He said that helping people find their inner strength and endurance as well as hone the physical was a source of happiness for him, but he also said that he volunteered some of his time to help feed the homeless. Spending time listening to their stories had enriched his life, and he hoped that it had done the same for them. He had said that connecting with people was where he found his happiness on a regular basis.

Noelle worked at a wilderness school and taught young people the fundamentals of living off the land. She said that happiness was never far away when she was in nature. She loved her work, feeling like she was teaching vital skills and an appreciation for the earth. She said that her struggle was with loneliness. Because of the nature of her work, she spent a lot of time with people who just passed in and out of her life. It was very rewarding, she had said, but sometimes she wished for more of a community. So, when Bethany had sent her an email asking if she'd want to join the old gang on this hike, she had arranged her schedule so she could go.

I was so lost in my thoughts that I jumped out of my skin when an alarm went off in my car signaling low tire pressure. The nearest town was still several miles away, so I kept going, hoping that my pressure was just low. But then I heard the change in the sound of the tires and knew I had to pull over. The mountain road was pretty narrow, and the shoulder wasn't wide enough for me to get all the way off the road. My mind raced, I didn't know whether I should keep going and hope I find a better place to pull off the road and risk damaging my wheel, or if I should just stop here and hope that no one crashed into me?

I turned on my hazard lights and pulled off the road as far as I could. I hadn't seen many other cars going by, so I hoped it wouldn't be too dangerous. *It's a good thing I have roadside assistance.* I thought, remembering how it had saved me so many times in the past. But, as I picked up my phone, I saw the glaring symbol for no service. I groaned. Calling for help was not going to be an option.

I stepped out of the car. The driver's side rear tire was totally flat and starting to shred. Fuck. I did have a little spare donut tire in the back, but I had never changed a tire before. *Well, looks like you're going to learn now.* I reminded myself that I was a strong independent woman and laughed. I had seen it done before, so hopefully it wouldn't be too difficult. I opened up the back and pulled out the tire iron, jack, and the spare tire. A car whizzed by me, blaring its horn, not even slowing as it swerved into the other lane to avoid me. I looked after it, tempted to flip them the bird. Not worth it. I sighed and got down on the ground to look underneath the car to see where I should align the jack. *This is not fun. I don't know how to do this.* My thoughts were taking a whiny turn.

I heard another car coming and sat up. This one was stopping. The SUV pulled over behind me and a man stepped out. "Do you need some help?" he asked.

He had such a kind face that I was instantly at ease. "Yes, I kinda really do. I told myself that I'm a strong independent woman, but I've never actually changed a tire by myself before."

He laughed, "I'm sure you are, but I'll show you how. Next time it'll be all yours. We need to put something in front of the tires first since we're on an incline. We don't want the car getting away from us."

We searched the mountain side for something that would work and came back with a few large branches that we wedged underneath the other tires. I watched while he loosened the lug nuts, jacked up the car, removed the tire, and replaced it with the spare.

"From Florida, I saw?" he asked as he finished tightening the last bolt.

"Yeah," I replied. "You?"

"Used to live in Florida too, but now I'm here. I retired from the Service Department with Ford a few years ago, but now I just rebuild classic cars and raise Chesapeake Bay Retrievers," he grinned at me as he stood up and dusted off his hands. "Alright, this should hold you for a little while, just get a replacement tire as soon as you can. Don't go back to Florida with this donut on."

"No, of course I wouldn't. Do you know a good place around here to get a new one?"

"Sorry, no. I actually live about an hour and a half from here, so I'm not certain what's nearby."

"Well, I can't even tell you how much I appreciate you stopping and helping me. Can I buy you dinner or coffee or something in town?" I asked, wanting to do something nice for him in return.

"No, no. It was my pleasure. I'm glad to help." He loaded the bad tire and the tools back into my car and shut the door.

"Thank you so much."

"Will you be okay from here on out?"

"Yes, I think so. You're my hero," I replied, gratefully.

He laughed, "Glad to be of service. Be safe."

He got back into his car and waved as he drove away.

As I continued down the mountain, my thoughts turned back to happiness. *The car getting a flat tire wasn't great. Being in the middle of nowhere was even worse. No signal on my phone was just the cherry on top as far as bad and stressful moments go. But then there was the guy that stopped to help. I don't think that would have happened if I'd been back in Orlando. In the city we tend to think that everyone is dangerous.* I sighed. *Life is so much better in the mountains.*

As I reached the bottom of the mountain, the roads got wider, the service returned to my phone, and I relaxed my grip on the steering wheel. I hadn't realized that I had been holding on so tightly. I could see a gas station coming up on my right, so I pulled in. I needed to google a tire place, and figure out where I was staying tonight.

After an exhaustive search and several phone calls, I found a few tire places in Bryson City, but I wouldn't be able to get to them before they closed. The earliest I was able to set up an appointment was for seven o'clock in the morning. There was a little bit of stress in the back of my mind as I did the math to figure out the drive time, knowing that I was supposed to meet Ethan at ten. It might be tight. I sighed and continued my search for a place to spend the night. A little country inn near the tire service place looked promising, so I booked my room.

The sun was starting to go down, but the temperature was still warm as I sat nestled up against a tree. It stood on the banks of the river behind the inn. My notebook was out and I was thinking about everything that had been talked about and experienced today. My heart felt full once again, it really had been an incredible day, despite the tire issue.

13. Being physically active and doing something in the service of others seems to be a common denominator for happiness in addition to being grateful and creating (in some form). I wrote in my notebook.

I found myself just staring off down the river, watching the fading light make shadows in the water. I sat there listening to the quiet roar that was normal for these rushing mountain rivers. Words weren't coming, so I closed the notebook. Maybe right now it was more important that I just existed. The temperature was dropping quickly, so I brought the notebook back to my hotel room and grabbed the extra blanket from the drawer.

Back outside under the tree, I cocooned myself in the blanket and closed my eyes. It was amazing how much more I heard with my eyes closed. I could hear the rushing water, but it had different sounds within it. There were birds and insects making sounds as they welcomed the dusk, the slight breeze rustling the leaves in the tree above me. I opened my eyes, seeking out the visuals of the sounds that I had focused on. The river hitting into the rocks and branches made the most noise, the big rock near me stopped enough of the water to make it splash sometimes. The birds and insects weren't visible, except in the occasional flight of a bird heading back to its nest.

What a perfect evening. I sat there quietly for a long time just enjoying the sunset, but when my eyes started drooping I decided there was nothing wrong with an early night. Tomorrow would be full.

CHAPTER 16

He was standing in the parking area waiting for me as my driver and I pulled in. My heart skipped, and the butterflies I'd been feeling all morning intensified.

"Hey," Ethan hugged me as I got out of the car. "You've had quite the adventure since I last saw you."

"Yeah," I replied, "I'm sorry if you had to wait long for me. I had the appointment for seven but they weren't done until almost nine. I had no idea it would take them that long to change my tire, otherwise I would have just left it until afterwards."

He had let go of me in the hug, but had somehow managed to keep my hand in his as I finished my rapid attempt at an apology.

"Willa, it's no big deal. I was happy to wait and it wasn't that long. I'm excited to spend the day with you and share one of my favorite hikes."

"Thank you," I hugged his arm appreciatively. "I'm excited too." I let go of his hand, "let me grab my bag real quick and thank this guy again for driving me down here."

I put on my small day pack, adjusting the weight for comfort, and waved once more to the driver. I turned back to Ethan smiling. "Ready?"

"As I'll ever be," he replied, grinning back at me.

We walked all day, pausing only briefly for short rests. The mountain miles felt so much longer than the miles I was accustomed to walking. My step counter usually told me that I walked between 5-10 miles every day, but this was rough and I knew I'd be feeling it tomorrow.

Conversation with Ethan felt like nothing I'd ever experienced before. It flowed so easily and naturally as we talked about our college days, how we got to where we were now, musical inspirations, and dreams for the future. There were times that we were silent, but even that did not feel awkward.

It was late by the time we finally got to Fontana Dam and set up camp.

We built a fire, and as we sat there enjoying the silence and the sounds of the night, I asked Ethan what he believed about happiness, and his opinion on how to have a happily ever after.

"I don't know that I necessarily believe in a happily ever after. There's too much sadness in the world," he replied. "But I do believe in choosing happiness when possible."

"I guess I mean having a happiness that comes from within. A happiness that makes it possible to break out into song for no reason," I said. "I know it sounds silly, but one of the happiest moments on this trip so far was dancing in the rain with you."

Ethan grinned, "That was definitely a high point for me too. I just believe you have to let yourself feel everything, Willa. Happiness that comes from within isn't feeling positive all the time," he replied. "Things can get really shitty." He continued, "People close to us die, and the emptiness and devastation that it brings isn't happy. People lose their jobs, their means of providing for themselves and their families, and that's not happy either. Sorrow, sadness, loss, even despair must be felt in their entirety. The difference I've found is that when you have joy at your core, you don't let yourself stop moving forward."

"Okay, I get what you're saying," I replied thoughtfully. "But, when you're in the depths of despair, I know from experience, moving forward isn't something you're really even cognizant of. You either don't want to move forward or you simply can't."

The fire crackled as one of the logs fell in and the smoke shifted, blowing a cloud into my face. Coughing, I waved my hand in front of my face to clear the smoke. I looked over at Ethan, and he was smiling at me.

"Don't laugh!" I protested, "I swallowed smoke!"

"I'm sorry," he said, his tone repentant, but I could still see his eyes twinkling in the firelight.

"I know," I said, "I'm such a city girl."

"It's alright. We'll make you a woodsman yet," he smiled at me.

I grinned appreciatively back at him. "So, anyway, like I was saying before that smoke so rudely interrupted me…"

Our eyes met again across the fire and we both chuckled.

"How do you expect someone that is in despair to keep moving forward and to even glimpse joy? Despair is really the very opposite of happiness."

Ethan paused a moment before responding, staring into the fire. "Much of what I've witnessed for that situation comes from my mom. I had an older brother who died when we were still kids."

"Oh my gosh. I'm so sorry," I said instinctively.

He nodded, then continued, "He misunderstood my mom, and didn't realize that when she said, 'Let's go' she was talking to me. I was holding her hand and I wanted to keep pressing the button on the crosswalk. I don't know how he didn't realize that there was a car coming up quickly, but he stepped out into the road. Mom screamed at him, but it was too late. I still hear the screeching brakes in my dreams sometimes."

"Oh my God. That's horrible. I'm so sorry."

"My mom was never the same after that. She could have easily blamed herself or me for the accident. I definitely blamed myself. But daily my mom would tell me that it wasn't anyone's fault. It wasn't mine, it wasn't hers, it wasn't the driver, and it wasn't Daniel's. It was an accident. She told me more often how much she loved me, how proud of me that she was. We would talk about our favorite moments with Daniel, keeping his memory fresh as time went by. You could tell by looking at her that a piece of her soul died that day with him, but she kept going. She seemed to get gentler and kinder as she got older. One day I asked her how she managed to keep going. Her response was this, she said, 'I keep going because you need me, our family needs me, even the world needs me. Nothing matters more than love. I decided that each moment is time given to me, whether I want it or not. Each interaction I have is one that can bring more love into the world. When your brother died I found that I couldn't bear the thought of people not knowing how important they were to this life. I had to choose, I could give up and turn inward, or live and embrace each moment of the life given to me and make a difference.'

It had a profound impact on my life and the person I was becoming to hear those words from her, and watch how she handled her grief. Everyone grieves differently, though, and I've found that it's important to let people feel everything that they're feeling. To put it in the form of a metaphor, emotions are like waves, and I think it's really important to learn how to surf so you aren't drowned by their overwhelming power."

He was silent for a minute, and then continued, "So, basically, for me, gratitude and an awareness of the life around us and in us provides a peace that bits of happiness can creep through. That is what gives us the foundation of joy deep in our soul that infiltrates our moments."

I sat there contemplating the fire as I thought about his story.

"That's such a powerful story. I'm so sorry for you and your family. I have a question about what you said about gratitude, though."

"Okay," Ethan responded, "what is it?"

"I don't want to say this wrong, or insensitively, but where did you find gratitude in the death of your brother? It's such a horrible thing and it seems to make light of it to find gratitude in it."

He didn't answer the question right away, and I looked at him across the fire, concerned that I had said that badly.

"I'm sorry-"

"No, no. I'm just thinking about how to respond," he interrupted. "It's not gratitude for the event itself, that is not a good thing. But finding things to be grateful for during times of despair is what I'm talking about. Did you ever read Pollyanna when you were a kid?"

"Of course I did," I exclaimed with mock indignation.

He chuckled and continued, "Remember her 'glad game'? She was always finding things to be glad about even when things were rough. I've just found that, like I was saying earlier, it's crucial to let yourself feel everything. But it's just as important to find the happy things that still exist even in our darkest moments. It's really an exercise for your mind. Some days it's almost impossible, and others you can find them without too much difficulty."

We were quiet for a few minutes, both of us just watching the fire.

"I really appreciate you telling me about your brother and your mom. It means a lot."

"Of course. I'm glad to share their stories," he replied.

"What your mom said about nothing mattering except for love and making sure that people know how important they are to this life. That's super powerful."

"Yeah. She's really the best."

It was late, and I knew we were both exhausted. Other hikers had joined us at the fire. Ethan had moved to sit next to me when they had arrived.

"Do you want to go out towards the dam and stargaze for a little while before we go to bed?" I whispered. I didn't want this day to end. Tomorrow he'd be getting back on the trail, and who knows when I would see him again.

"Yes. That's a great idea," he responded, standing up. He'd been holding my hand and reached for my other one, pulling me to my feet. I could tell he wanted to kiss me at that moment, but I just hugged him. I suddenly felt shy and didn't want strangers observing our first kiss.

I grabbed a blanket from my car as we passed it looking for a good spot to stargaze.

"How about here?" We were overlooking the lake and the night sky seemed to stretch on forever.

"It's perfect," I agreed, laying out the blanket.

We lay there close together in silence, just looking up at the stars. I was serenely happy. I turned my head slightly to look at his face, he looked back at me.

"What are you thinking?" he asked me.

"Just how happy I am at this moment."

"It is a pretty perfect moment, isn't it," he agreed. He shifted his arm under my head and I nestled in closer to him.

"It's one of those ones that you never want to end."

"Well, don't think about it ending. Look at that!" Pointing at the stars above us, "doesn't that look like the McDonalds symbol?"

I laughed. "Yeah, I guess so. I was looking over at that one," I pointed at the stars a little to the west of us. "It looks like Darth Vader." We both cracked up laughing.

His other hand touched my waist and I jumped.

"Oh, sorry."

"No, no, I'm just ticklish," I responded.

"Oh, you are, are you?" There was a mischievous twinkle in his eyes as I glanced over at him.

He turned over towards me and began tickling me in earnest. Laughing and wriggling, there was only one way I could stop this. Turning my head to his, I reached up and pulled his face down to mine and kissed him. He immediately stopped tickling, totally distracted by my lips on his.

CHAPTER 17

I was sitting inside a coffee shop the next morning, my mind racing. I could feel my face blushing just thinking about last night. I held my hands to my face to cool it down. *Stop behaving like a high schooler.* I told myself severely. *You're a grown ass woman and are allowed to have a little romance.* I sighed. *Last night was so perfect. He was perfect.*

But now I needed to figure out my next couple of days, and do some writing. I had a lot that needed processing in the Happiness diary.

14. Loving yourself - Bethany said that it was critical to happiness and relied hugely on integrity. I don't think I've ever thought about integrity before, not using that word anyway. I've certainly known people that have not been true to their word. People that can say one thing one moment, but then act in the complete opposite. After these conversations, I can see that they really didn't like themselves. I bet that the guilt and shame of not being true to yourself or your word would build up eventually until you felt that all the time. Since I'm going with the Disney vibe, all the heroes and heroines in those stories are definitely noble, honorable, and kind. Full of integrity.

I drew hearts along the edges of the paper as I considered what I wanted to write about next, then drew a smiley face.

15. Contentedness - Mark's version of happiness was based on being content with what he had. He said that he didn't feel like he needed to have the next best thing, or achieve the traditional definitions of success. He had realized that he could be happy even with very little. When his wife had left him, he had to realize that he was not a failure, and that the single life had a peace about it that hadn't been present in his life, especially at the end of his relationship. He had said that being content with a little made it so that he was able to put his employees and customers first, and was able to reward bonuses and discounts out of his profits. He said because of these fair business practices, he had developed a bunch of loyal employees and customers.

I wonder what I can do to cultivate this in my own life. I love that he has been able to step away from the capitalist point of view.

16. Community

Noelle mentioned community, and how the lack of it really was the main source of any unhappiness that she felt. I don't think I've ever considered community as a bit of happiness. But I can't imagine living somewhere where I didn't know people. Even though it's Orlando, I see people I know every day, even if it's just on a trip to the store or a walk in the park. There's people I went to school with, regulars at my salon, people that I knew from past jobs. There's other regulars from places that my friends and I frequent, there's just always someone to say hi to. I can't imagine feeling isolated like Noelle said that she did, always feeling like a stranger, and having to make new friends every year.

I looked up from my notebook and just watched. The coffee shop was bustling with a steady flow of customers. There was a woman seated on the other side of the coffee table in another armchair. She was staring into her coffee cup.

"Can I ask you a question?"

The woman looked up at me and nodded.

"I'm working on a project exploring happiness and what it looks like for different people. I was wondering where you find your happiness?"

The woman's eyes filled with tears. "I'm not the best person to ask right now. My life has completely gone to shit, and I have no idea what to do, let alone how to be happy."

"Oh, I'm so sorry," I replied, sympathy etched in my tone. "I don't know if I can help at all, but do you want to talk about it? Comfort of strangers and all that?"

The woman looked dubious, "I don't know, it's kind of a lot."

"Well, I don't mean to pry. I just hate to see you in pain and not offer to at least listen."

"I appreciate that. Maybe it would be good to talk about it. I don't know."

"Well, my name is Willa, I'm not from here, I live in Orlando. Honestly, I've been feeling so lost in my own life that I took a trip up here to see if I could figure out my own answers."

"It's a relief to know I'm not the only one, I'm Daisy." She paused, letting out a sigh. "I guess I just thought at this point of my life everything would be smooth sailing." She smiled wryly. "But it's not. I'm 45 years old, my husband left me recently for a 23-year-old, and my son, who has been my world, hasn't spoken to me in weeks. My boss told me last week that my job is being phased out at work, and that my options were to either transfer to a lower paying position, or to move out to the west coast. But the west coast position would be doing everything I hate, and it's only temporary. Plus, it's away from everything and everyone I know." She took a deep breath and let it out slowly. "So, I've been looking for another job with the limited bandwidth that I have. I've also been trying to pick up the pieces from my failed marriage, and adjust to being single again. But I don't know who I am anymore. My son is in his first year of college and only contacts me when he needs something, so I feel used. But then I feel guilty because I shouldn't feel used, because he's my son, and I should give him what he needs, right?"

It was so much. She had let all of that out without even pausing to breathe.

I reached over and took her hand. She had been squeezing the arm of the chair as if it was the only thing keeping her afloat. Daisy burst into tears and I tightened my grip. I didn't know what else to do, I just didn't want her to feel like she was alone.

"That's not even all of it," she continued, using her free hand to wipe away her tears. "I had to put my dog down yesterday because he wasn't responding to the treatments for his cancer anymore. He was suffering and I couldn't bear to keep watching. I forced myself to get out of the house today and come here, but I feel like I can't do any of the things that I would normally do. The weight of everything feels too enormous, and I just want to disappear. But would that even solve anything?"

There were tears in my eyes too by the time she finished. She took her hand away from mine as she reached for her purse to get a tissue.

"Daisy, I'm so sorry," I said, my heart breaking for her.

"Yeah. Me too," She sighed. "I just don't have anything happy to tell you right now, I wish I did."

"Can I tell you about some of the things I've been learning? I don't think I have all the answers, but maybe it would at least be interesting to hear what I've learned from other people on my trip?"

Daisy blew her nose and nodded. "At this point I'm desperate for anything. I can't continue like this. I'm usually a strong independent woman, but, right now, I just want to curl up under a rock."

"So, I met this man Ethan the other day, and we were talking about how absolutely hard life can be. He said that he thinks it's important to feel everything. That there's nothing wrong with feeling despair and uncertainty, so long as we keep moving forward," I began. I didn't know what I was doing. I didn't have the answer yet, but I couldn't just sit here and say nothing. *Maybe this is what Ethan's mom meant when she told him that she had to make sure that people knew they were loved.* "One of the first things that came up was gratitude. I met some older women at a cafe down near Saluda, and they said that gratitude was key to happiness. A few others agreed. One of them said that even when things were down and out, it was important to look for the things that you could be happy about in the moment you were in, inane as they might be. For instance, at this moment, I'm glad to be talking to you. This coffee is totally hitting the spot right now, and even more innocuous, I'm grateful to be breathing. He said that just doing that takes you out of the weight of everything, and makes you focus on the moments. Honestly, I haven't done much of it yet, so I'm just telling you what he told me, but I think it makes sense."

"I guess so..." Daisy agreed dubiously.

"When I was up at Fontana Dam, I met a hiking group, and one of the women there was convinced that the core of happiness had to do with believing that you're loved. Even if, or maybe especially if, it was based on loving yourself. She really emphasized how important it was to train your brain out of negative self-talk."

"I definitely don't feel loved by the people in my life." She regarded me thoughtfully for a minute before continuing, "I always thought that I had a healthy amount of love for myself, but I think losing my husband really messed me up. I always thought that he and I would be together forever, but..." Daisy's tears started flowing again. "A few weeks ago, he was packing for a business trip, and he told me that he wasn't coming back. He'd met someone else. He said that he felt like he was suffocating with me."

"Oh no."

"I don't know, maybe we'd gotten too comfortable in our routines, and with our son off to college…"

"I'm so sorry. I can't even imagine how devastating that would be."

"My career was always a big part of my life, but the rest of the time was devoted to being the best mom and wife I could be, at least that's what I told myself. Apparently, I went wrong somewhere. I'm not sure where I lost myself, but now it's like I have to figure everything out all over again."

"Do you think talking to a professional would help?"

Daisy sighed. "Yes, probably. But I've never talked to a therapist before, and it's really intimidating."

I nodded. Obviously I'd struggled with the idea of talking to a life coach. But I said, "I think maybe it would be worth it, though. I have a friend who went through a bad divorce, and she said that therapy was the only thing that kept her going. You're dealing with more than anyone should ever have to deal with and in such quick succession too."

"Yeah," she agreed, "you're right. That's probably what I should do, I've just been avoiding it."

"I wish I had a way to help you myself."

"You did help. It was good to talk to you, so thank you for asking."

Daisy got up to leave. "Can I ask you, it seems like a weird thing to do, but can I get your number?"

I laughed, "Of course you may."

She blushed, "I would love to hear what else you discover by the end of your trip."

I tore a sheet out of my happiness notebook and wrote down my name and number. "You are worthy of love. You are beautiful. You are strong. You are amazing. I'm so glad I met you." I scribbled at the bottom. I folded the paper and handed it to her.

"Thanks again for talking," Daisy said, taking the paper and turning away.

"Bye."

I sat there for a long minute thinking. *Daisy definitely had a rough go of it right now. I can't even imagine having a husband leave me after 20 years, that alone would be earth shattering, let alone everything else she was dealing with.* I sighed and gathered up my things. *Lunch and then a hike.*

CHAPTER 18

I brought my notebook into the restaurant. I wanted to do a little more writing. As I sat down at the bar, the man next to me introduced himself. "Hey! I'm Steve." He was smiling broadly.

Immediately I felt my guard go up. "Hi Steve, I'm Willa."

The bartender came over and asked if I wanted a drink. I asked for a menu and ordered a mojito.

"So, are you here on vacation?" Steve asked.

I hesitated, I really didn't want to talk to him at all. That look he'd given me when I sat down, the creepy once over from head to toe hadn't gone unnoticed. He didn't look like he belonged in this little mountain town. But I had decided to talk to strangers on this trip, so I replied.

"I'm just traveling through, trying to figure out some things." Still being evasive, there was just something about that look in his eyes that made me so uncomfortable.

"Things like what?"

"I'm trying to figure out how to have a happiness that comes from within."

"You're thinking too much, girl." He winked, "I can give you happiness within."

I almost hit him. The leering smile, the wink, it was too much.

"No, Steve," I replied, sternly, "that's not the type of happiness I'm talking about. I have someone in my life, I'm not looking for a good time."

"Your loss."

"I'm sure." There might have been a touch of sarcasm in my tone.

"I'm serious," he continued, "You want purpose? Pleasure, babe. That's where happiness is."

"Are you serious?"

"Sex, drugs, and rock and roll, what more do you need?"

"Oh my God."

"Yeah. I'd have you screaming that!"

"You're being gross. I already told you that I have someone."

"What he doesn't know won't hurt him. Come on, baby. You'll forget all this nonsense when I show you what's up." He winked at me and glanced down at his crotch.

I stared at him, horrified. "It's not nonsense, Steve. I think it's time for me to go."

I stood up and went over to the hostess.

"May I sit at a table?"

"Is that man bothering you?"

"Honestly, yes. He's being gross."

"I'm so sorry. I'll tell the manager. But here, come sit over here." She led me to a table.

"I'm so sorry about that, honey. Men are the worst."

"It's alright, it's not your fault. Not all men are terrible," I replied thinking of Ethan, "But that sort are really gross."

The waitress came over and I ordered my lunch. I could see Steve's back from where I was sitting. I can't deny the sense of satisfaction I felt when I saw the manager go over to him with his bill and send him away. Steve argued and protested loudly as the manager escorted him out the door.

When the manager came back inside, he came straight over to my table. "I am so sorry about that ma'am. We have a zero tolerance policy for harassment of any kind, and you should have never been subjected to that. The bartender heard what he said to you and informed me. That man will never be allowed back in this establishment."

"I don't think there's any way you could have known or done anything about it before it happened," I replied, smiling up into his concerned face. "I thought about smacking that leer off his face, but I decided it wouldn't solve anything. Besides, he'd probably like it."

"Yeah, probably." The manager grinned back at me, obviously relieved to see that I wasn't mad and holding him responsible. "I've got your lunch, though, so don't worry about your bill."

"Oh thank you! But you don't have to do that," I protested.

"It's alright. I've got it." He turned away and then looked back, "Marci is waiting on you, right?"

"Yeah, I think that's her name."

"Have her come get me before you leave, and I'll walk you out to your car, just in case that guy is still hanging around out there somewhere."

"Oh shit," I hadn't even thought of that possibility. "Yeah, I definitely will. Thanks."

I opened my notebook and continued where I left off.

17. What a weird day this has been already. Sharing what I learned with Daisy felt really good. I hope it helps her. This interaction with Steve just now was crazy. I don't even know what to say about it right now.

18. Ethan and I talked about so much it's hard to know what to say. Some of the major points he brought up were that happiness is just an emotion, and it's okay and even important to feel other emotions also. I loved his metaphor about emotions being like waves, and how it's important to learn how to surf so that you aren't overwhelmed. He said that it's important to keep moving forward and to find the happy moments even in the midst of bad things.

He's so good at staying in the moment. I hope I learn to be better at that. I really can't wait to spend more time with him.

My lunch arrived, so I closed my notebook and ate. The manager and I didn't see any sign of Steve when we walked out to my car a little while later, much to my relief.

I had programmed The Boogerman Trail as my next stop on my GPS. The trail was listed at number 2 in the best ranked trails around Maggie Valley. It said that it would take about four hours to complete, which I felt like was the perfect way to spend my afternoon. I thought about calling Gina as I drove and telling her about the encounter with Steve. But I decided against it. Reception was spotty, I'd tell her when I got home, along with all the other stories I'd have for her.

The drive was beautiful, my windows were down and the music up. Even a man like Steve couldn't mess up a day like this.

I had been on the trail for a little more than an hour when I heard footsteps behind me. Turning, I saw a man gaining on me quickly. I paused and stepped to the side to let him pass.

"Thanks," he murmured as he passed me.

I smiled and continued more slowly behind him. It was probably 30 minutes later that I heard more footsteps and, glancing back, I saw him again.

"How did I pass you?" I asked, shocked. "Or are you lapping me?"

"Oh, no, you passed me." He smiled back at me. "I stepped off the trail to get some pictures and video."

"Oh cool. Is it for anything in particular?"

"Yeah, I run a hiking blog, so I'm getting content for it."

"That's awesome." I was impressed. I never really understood how people made a living off of blogging. It was hard enough for me to remember to take pictures and upload content for my hair on Instagram. Luckily, we had a social media team who handled most of that for us.

"I'm Jim," he said, stretching out his hand for me to shake.

"Willa," I replied. "Nice to meet you. You'll have to give me the link to your blog."

"Yeah, of course." There was a pause as we continued walking. "So, what do you do?" he asked. He seemed content to walk along with me now, instead of trying to pass by.

"I do hair back in Orlando."

"Just up here on vacation?"

"Yeah, kinda," I replied.

He looked over at me, his gaze sardonic. "Kinda vacation?"

I chuckled, "Yeah. It is a vacation, but I'm up here because I'm on a happiness quest."

"What does that mean?" he asked.

"It just means that I'm trying to figure out what it means to live happily ever after." He snorted, so I rushed to explain it better. "I just want to live happily, really."

"Well, I mean, good luck?"

"Why do you say it like that?" I asked him.

"Because, Willa, life isn't happy. It's navigating one despair after another. You get through one shit pile and then another one is dumped on top of you. Fairy tales and especially their endings are silly. They only create a false sense of hope in those who refuse to acknowledge reality."

I stared at him. I hadn't been expecting that. "Ouch." I paused to consider how I wanted to respond, "Are you never happy then?"

"Sure I am, sometimes. In the rare moments between the shit. I'm not trying to be mean, I just think that you going on this happiness quest is a colossal waste of time," he replied. "Is there anything about your life that has gone like you wanted it to? Or even think about it this way, why do you think you're entitled to happiness? What makes you different from the rest of us?"

"Wow." I was startled and hurt by the harshness in his tone. "I don't think that I'm entitled to happiness, I just think that life shouldn't be boring and sad. I want there to be a purpose to my life."

"Ah. There is the fundamental flaw in your plan. There is no purpose to life."

"How can you even say that?" I protested.

"Easily. Humanity is a parasite, or a virus if you'd rather. We're destroying this world with no thought or care because it doesn't affect us personally in the moment. This culture only cares about celebrities and money. If we weren't here, the planet would be in great shape, it could probably even heal itself from the damage we've done. Animals wouldn't live in cages or outside of their environments. There would be a natural circle of life. Evolution wouldn't be stunted or modified."

"You're not wrong," I said thoughtfully, "but we are here, we are alive. There has to be a reason."

He scoffed, "Yeah, no. There isn't."

"But, Jim," I protested, "I can't get on board with there not being a reason. I guess it ties back to this book I listened to on the way up here, it can't just be 'it is what it is' it has to be 'it is what you make of it.' We have to make there be a purpose to our life. And maybe, just maybe, we can change the world."

He shook his head but was silent.

We walked on in silence for a while, the only noise coming from our footsteps and breathing. My thoughts raced, I wanted to convince him that it wasn't a waste to be alive, that happiness was a worthy goal. But then my thoughts went to how noisy our steps sounded in the silence of the woods, and I giggled.

Jim looked over at me, surprised. "What's funny?"

"I was just thinking about how Native Americans used to walk silently through the woods, and here we are just tramping away, crunching leaves and sticks, and kicking rocks…" I kicked a small stone off the path for dramatic effect.

He gave me a small smile, "Yeah, we're not going to sneak up on anything."

"Do you ever imagine what it would have been like walking through the forest back in the old days?"

He shook his head, "I don't think I've ever thought about it before. But, it would have been a lot more dangerous, for sure."

We walked along, no more talking, and I could tell we were both being quieter with our footsteps. Maybe he too was now imagining the old days before these trails were developed and the wonder of exploring places seen before by only animals.

"It's just so pointless!" Jim exclaimed.

I jumped, startled out of my thoughts. "What is?"

"This 'Happiness Quest' you say you're on. Don't you see what a waste of time it is?"

"I don't agree," I argued. "I've met such incredible people and learned so much about happiness and living happily."

"But it's bullshit, Willa. Lies people tell themselves to keep moving forward. You're on an emotional high stemming from vacation and doing things outside your comfort zone. Once you get back to your real life, do you actually think that it will continue?"

The vehemence of his tone was so angry that I stopped walking and stared back at him.

"First of all, why are you talking to me like that? Why are you angry at me? And honestly, Jim, there's no reason for you to be so hateful. You just met me."

He let out a laugh, further shocking me. "Oh, don't take it personally. I hate everything and everyone, including myself. But I hate the lies we tell ourselves most of all."

"I don't even know what to do with that." My eyes were still wide as I continued to stare back at him.

"Well, after you get back to Orlando, remember what I said."

"I will. I'm going to prove you wrong. I don't know how, but I'm going to."

Jim rolled his eyes, "Okay, call me when you do. I'll be waiting."

"You think I won't. I will. I refuse to accept this pessimistic worldview you have. Yes, things are shitty. Yes. But happiness isn't a lie, it is achievable, and I will figure out how to live a happy life. I'll call you when I have nailed down the specifics and then you have to promise me to test it out too."

He sighed. "Fine, Willa. You have a deal."

"Good," I grinned at him and he reluctantly smiled back.

We continued in silence for a few minutes, "So…"

"Yeah?" he asked.

"Why the hiking blog?"

"Gives me the opportunity to be outside and travel. I can't sit at a desk for long, I get bored, and like I said earlier, I hate people."

"Okay, I'm curious now, doesn't your blog get people to go out in nature? Doesn't that go against your theory of the awfulness of people and their effects on the environment?"

"Yes," Jim agreed. "But my blog is actually called Don't Fuck It Up. Probably half of my posts point out the destruction caused by humans, and the posts that I make about the beauty of nature I always end with 'Don't Fuck It Up'."

I laughed, "I love it. That's so perfect. But I do have a question, by doing this - traveling, writing, exploring nature - isn't that your purpose? You do seem to love it."

"Purpose implies destiny. A design in this chaos. A higher power. I refute all of that nonsense. I do what I do because it's the least shitty option that I've found. Do you think that what you do is your purpose?"

I hesitated. "Honestly, I'd never really even considered having a purpose before this trip. But it comes up pretty frequently in conversations. It is something I want to give some more thought to, though."

CHAPTER 19

It wasn't until after I was settled into my bed that evening that I started going over my conversation with Jim again in my head.

What was my purpose? So many people have mentioned it. Is my purpose to make people feel good about themselves with their hair like Ethan mentioned?

I wasn't ready to discount having a purpose like Jim. I did believe in destiny and a higher power. Maybe that was just wishful thinking on my part, but my soul cried out for more, and that's why I was here on this trip.

I drifted off to sleep.

I didn't wake up the next morning until almost noon. I was back at the KOA in Cherokee. I had decided that I wanted a few days of quiet to have time to really think about everything before I headed back to Florida.

I looked at my phone, I had a text from Ethan, and my heart skipped a beat as I opened it.

"Good morning beautiful, I'm walking now, I don't have service, but I am hoping this reaches you some time this morning. Do you think you'll still be up here six days from now? I'm supposed to meet my friend Tim and his wife at Hot Springs, and, if you were still here, we could maybe have another day together. I just keep thinking about you because you're amazing. I think you're smart and sexy. I love that you danced in the rain with me, that you think about deep things, and that you try things outside your comfort zone. Anyway, I just figured I'd ask, just in case."

My heart leapt, but then sank. *I hadn't planned on being up here almost a week from now... but could I?* I opened my scheduler.

My mind raced. *Should I go home and come back?* I hadn't really thought that I would be gone for 2 weeks. It felt like such a long time to be gone. I was used to taking an extra day here and there for my days off, not two weeks in a row. Especially two weeks by myself. *But I would get another day with Ethan... Wasn't this trip supposed to be about figuring out happiness outside of men, though?* I sighed.

I felt lost all of a sudden. I wanted to see him again, but there was the other side of me that was protesting. I texted Christy.

"Hey! Do you have time to talk?"

"Give me a minute and I'll call you," she responded.

I looked up the town of Hot Springs while I waited. *Crazy that it will take me about two hours to drive what was six days of hiking. Granted, he's climbing mountains, but still.*

My phone vibrated.

"Hey, thanks for calling me," I answered the phone.

"Of course!" Christy exclaimed, "What's up?"

"So, I met this guy up here the other day..." I told her the story of how I met Ethan, the stories that he'd shared, and of our instant connection. "So, he just asked me to meet up with him again in a few days, and I want to, but I can't help but think that this is sidetracking me from my goal of finding happiness without a guy. So, part of me thinks that I should say no. What do you think?"

Christy didn't answer right away. "Does it feel like you're basing your happiness on him? Or is he just adding to it? I've found that some of the most profound magic in life comes when opportunities arise. Stepping forward in uncertainty, but with faith that the universe, God, destiny, whatever you subscribe to, has your best interests at heart can actually pave the way for happiness too."

"I just don't think I have this all figured out yet. I feel like I have a bunch of the building blocks now from all of the people that I've met. But it doesn't feel like it's all tied together yet. So, I'm scared that I don't know for sure if he's adding to my happiness or if I'm going to fall into the same old rhythms. I was not trying to find love on this trip."

I could hear Christy smiling as she said, "Is he a love already?"

I felt my face flush. "No, I don't know. But maybe."

"Well, my opinion is that you should go for it. I think that you are dedicated to finding that joy deep within you. So when something so magical happens, follow it. See what happens."

"Okay. Thanks, Christy," my heart had hoped this is what she would say.

We hung up and I went back to my scheduler.

I moved around some more appointments. My next month was going to be crazy busy, but worth it for this.

I texted Ethan, "I'm moving some things around so that I can be. Good morning!"

It didn't show up as delivered so I knew he was out of his service area again.

What the hell was I going to do for the next few days? I had been thinking that I would go home tomorrow, but now what?

I reached for my notebook and headed outside. The little porch on my cabin had a swing and I settled in.

19. There has been so much lately, things I haven't taken the time to write down, positives and negatives.

Happiness does look different for everyone. Steve, the creeper from the bar, had proclaimed that Sex, Drugs, and Rock and Roll were his tenets to happiness. I wonder if those things actually did make him happy, or if they just numbed the other feelings?

Jim said there was no purpose to life, that happiness was bullshit, and the pursuit of it was a waste of time. I will prove him wrong. I mean, he said he didn't like people so he spent his time away from them. Yet, he was the one that joined me walking on the trail. And he also chooses to spend his time around things that he likes. I wish I had thought of that while we were talking, I wonder what he would have said to that.

He said that I was happy because I was outside my comfort zone. He probably wasn't wrong about that. People do seem to naturally gravitate towards their comfort zones, and while it might not be happy, at least it's comfortable. That was my situation back home for sure. Daisy's situation, too. Her marriage and relationship with her son, both were comfortable, but lacking. Maybe due to communication. I wonder when she and her husband fell out of love and how it happened. God, I hope that never happens to me.

The pattern really seems to stay the same no matter who I talk to, with the exception of Steve (and Jim of course). Happiness is found in helping people or positive input in the community. It is also important to be active and creative. And then, maybe most important of all, I need to cultivate a mind that focuses on gratitude and being content.

I found myself embracing solitude for the next couple of days. My mornings were spent sipping coffee and moving slowly. I'd pack a lunch and go hiking. The afternoons were full just sitting by rivers and waterfalls, setting up my hammock in the forest, and listening to the animals and birds interact. I had nowhere to be and no time schedule. In the evenings, I'd go to a local bar for dinner. No one tried to talk to me, and I didn't go out of my way to talk to anyone either. It wasn't that I felt like I was done figuring out happiness, I just felt like I had taken in so much information on other people's path to happiness, now I needed to figure out mine.

The afternoon of the fourth day I wrote more in my journal as I contemplated my own life back in Orlando.

If I look at my life just the way that it is, my happiest moments are when I'm spending time with my mom or my friends. And also when my clients looked in the mirror when I was done with their hair and I saw the smile grow on their faces. But, other than that, I can't really think of times when my heart feels as full as it does now. There isn't a lot of unhappiness, there's just a whole lot of blah. Neither happy nor unhappy. What are some things that I can change, knowing what I know now?

My reverie was interrupted by the sound of someone coming towards me.

"That's my spot! Leave! You need to get out of here! Who do you think you are?" There were a few expletives thrown in. I wasn't sure if the person was talking to me or to someone else, but I got out of the hammock, just in case. My notebook fell on the ground in my hurry. The yelling continued as he approached me, but I still wasn't sure if he was talking to me or voices in his head.

The man didn't look like he had been a part of civilization for quite some time. My heart was in my throat, I had no way of protecting myself if he did attack me. He never looked directly at me, though, when he was yelling. So, instead of running, I hesitated.

"You want me to leave, sir?" I called up to him as he scrambled down the trail to my spot by the river.

"I don't care about you," he replied, this time looking at me directly. He was almost to where I was. "What are you doing out here? It's not safe. They might attack you."

I unhooked my hammock and started rolling it up. "I didn't know."

He picked up my journal, and looked inside. "Happiness? What have you got to be unhappy about? Did your parents beat you within an inch of your life and send you out in the dead of winter without shoes or a coat?"

I unhooked the other side of the hammock and stuffed it into its bag.

"No sir." I tried to keep my voice calm.

"Were you picked up by the police and sent to jail because of how you look? I was never guilty of anything that they said. I was raped in there, but no one cared." His voice was raw and angry.

"I'm sorry that happened to you."

"You don't know what unhappiness is, girl." He handed me the journal and turned away with a sigh. "I could tell you stories that would break your heart a million times over. You have no idea." He waded out into the water, then suddenly yelled "Shut the fuck up! No one asked you!"

I finished packing up and turned away, scrambling up the trail, my heart in my throat.

He is right, though. There are people out there that have it way worse than I do. I felt a wave of guilt rush over me. *People facing hunger, people getting harassed and abused, people who have never had a chance at a good life, and here I am whining about my privileged, well taken care of life.*

I called Christy as soon as I got back to my car. There were tears streaming down my face as I explained what had just happened and how the reality of it hit me.

"Oh Willa!" she exclaimed. "That's a lot. I'm glad you're okay, though, that sounds like it was scary."

I wiped my eyes, trying not to smear my makeup. "It was. He didn't do anything to me, and he wasn't yelling at me, I don't think, but I don't know. Maybe he was harmless, I couldn't tell. But, Christy, he was right. I don't have any right to be unhappy."

"That's not true. You can't compare your realities. What you feel is what you feel. It's good to be aware and grateful for the ease of our lives. But the discontent you were feeling is bringing you to the person you were meant to be. If you weren't meant for more, you wouldn't be feeling the way you do."

"I appreciate what you're saying, but I can't feel like that right now." I said, the adrenaline, the guilt, the relief, had left me feeling emotionally exhausted. I didn't even know what to think, let alone how to feel.

"That's more than okay," Christy assured me. "Try not to wallow, and when you can, write down all the things you're grateful for. Everyone is entitled to happiness, whether they've been dealt a bad hand in life or not. Keep searching for yours."

I drove back to my campsite and curled up in my bed. Christy said not to wallow, but I needed to. *The homeless, the mentally ill, drug addicts, people under the poverty line, people with bad home lives, single parents, people of color, or those with alternative lifestyles or identities…* The more I thought, the list seemed never ending. *How could I complain about my comfortably middle class life? Things hadn't necessarily been easy, but they certainly hadn't been that hard. Maybe Jim was right after all. What right had I to expect a happily ever after when there was so much that was terrible and hard in the world.*

I cried until I couldn't any longer, then fell asleep.

I didn't wake up until well after midnight. A text from Ethan was waiting for me when I glanced at my phone.

"Hey, you've been on my mind. Really excited to see you. I hope you're having a great adventure and I can't wait to hear about it."

I smiled and sent a heart-eyes emoji. "It's really been something. Great overall until yesterday, kinda feel like I lost my bearings. Hoping to get myself back together in the morning. Looking forward to seeing you too. One more day!"

I rolled over and went back to sleep feeling better.

CHAPTER 20

I pulled up to the hotel in Hot Springs that I'd booked for the next two nights. There was an excitement and a touch of nervousness that I couldn't stifle. Ethan had said that his friend Chris, who had picked up his car in Wesser, would actually be coming up for a short visit this evening, bringing him some supplies. Chris and his wife lived in Asheville and were some of his best friends. It felt weird to be meeting his best friends already, but, at the same time, nothing was traditional about this whole situation. All I knew was that I'd been counting down the minutes until I got to see him again. I smiled, thinking again about that first kiss under the stars.

I went inside to check in. The proprietor informed me that it would be another hour or two before our room was ready, but that I was welcome to hang out in the courtyard. "Otherwise," he said, smiling kindly, "There's several cute little shops along the street for you to check out. But, if you're not in the mood for shopping, the river is just past the railway tracks. There is a trail that runs along the banks, and it's a gorgeous walk."

"Awesome. Thanks. I know the Appalachian trail comes through town here somewhere, where is the south trail head?" I asked, thinking I could potentially meet Ethan there. *Or maybe that would be too weird and stalkery.*

"Yes, it does." He was still smiling at me. "If you go out to your right, follow the road straight. Don't turn right at the fork. You'll see the access off to your right just past the Blue Ridge Hiking Trail-er."

"Perfect. Thanks again." I turned and headed out the door.

Hot Springs, North Carolina was one of the tiniest towns I'd ever visited, businesses lined the main street for a few blocks, but that was it. There was nothing else. It was incredibly quaint, though, the little tourist shops geared toward visitors and especially the hikers that passed through regularly.

"Hey," I texted Ethan, "I made it to Hot Springs, but the room won't be ready for another hour or two. What's your ETA?"

I walked towards my car, not quite sure if I should stick around here or go exploring.

My phone vibrated with a call coming in. Ethan. "Hey!" I couldn't keep a smile off my face as I answered.

"Hey you! I have service, so I figured I'd call instead of text."

Just the sound of his voice had my heart beating wildly. "Oh good, I like phone calls." I knew I was smiling like a silly school girl, but I realized I didn't care.

"Good," I could hear the smile in his voice too. "I think I'm about an hour out, I made good time this morning."

"Awesome," I paused for a second as my mind raced. "What if I were to walk towards you down the trail from here?"

"You don't have to do that!" he exclaimed.

"What if I want to?" I teased.

"Willa, I absolutely cannot wait to see you, so if you want to start walking my way, I'm not going to stop you."

"Good," I replied, "because I'm dying to see you too." I opened the car door, "just grabbing my little pack, and I'm headed towards you."

"You're so adorable."

I giggled, I couldn't help it. "You're not so bad yourself. I'll see you soon."

We hung up, and I quickly walked in the direction the hotel man had told me to go.

It was a little more than 30 minutes later when I rounded a bend in the trail and saw Ethan coming towards me. A brilliant smile lit up his face as he saw me too. My pace quickened to close the distance between us. A brief thought flashed through my brain wondering if I should just play it cool and wait for him to get to me. But I discarded it immediately. I didn't want to play games with him. I wanted him to know that I was excited to see him. My brief worry disappeared completely when I saw that he quickened his pace as well. He held out his hands towards me, and I grasped them as soon as I was close enough. He pulled me in for a tight hug, and then turned his face down to mine and kissed me for a long minute. I swear I saw stars by the time he let me go. I smiled happily at him. "Hey you."

"Hey yourself," he replied, grinning back at me. "I'm sorry if I stink, but I'll take a shower as soon as we get to the room, I promise."

"No, you're fine." He did smell like sweat, but I didn't mind. I was a little bit sweaty now too.

He held out his hand for mine and I happily obliged.

"So. How's your adventure going? We haven't talked much about it since the last time I was with you and I got a little worried when I saw your text yesterday morning."

"Yeah, there've been other things to talk about," I smiled mischievously up at him, not wanting to get serious right away. We hadn't been able to do a whole lot of talking this week, a few texts here and there, but he hadn't had much service.

"You're right," He teased, winking at me. I felt myself blushing again. But then continued seriously, "but what has been going on?" The genuine interest in his tone warmed my heart. It felt so nice to know that this was important to him also.

I told him about the man by the river and my spiral because of it. His grip on my hand had tightened during parts of the story. I hadn't realized how nice it would be to feel like someone cared enough to be protective.

"Can I just say something real quick?" he asked when I told him about the tears caused by my realizations.

I nodded.

"I'm so glad you're safe, first. That could have had a very different outcome." He kissed my hand.

I don't think I'd ever had anyone kiss my hand before. It was such a possessive gesture, and I realized I didn't mind it one bit.

"I totally understand how you got thrown for a loop. I felt the same when I watched Mayor of Kingstown. We don't realize how good we have it, and while we know that life is bad for some, I don't think we really see it until it's in our faces. All that being said, though, I don't think you should compare your realities."

"Christy said the same thing." I told him about my conversation with her.

"Were you able to come to that same conclusion when you were able to think about it later?" he asked.

"Honestly? I haven't worked through it very much. In theory, yes, everyone is entitled to happiness, so of course I can be looking for mine. But, on the flip side, I feel this huge amount of guilt because a lot of people don't have it as good as I do. What right do I have to feel the way that I do?"

Ethan was silent for a moment. "Remember that conversation that you had with the guy who talked about standing at the ocean at night, feeling the water on his toes, and seeing nothing but the broad expanse of sea and the universe of stars in the sky? Remember how he said that when he would do that, he'd realize how small his own importance was in the grand scheme of everything?"

I nodded again, not sure where he was going with this train of thought.

"I think that the reverse in this case is more true for you. There is so much going on in the world, but you really only have control over your own self and your feelings. You were feeling blah about life for a myriad of reasons, totally valid ones at that. You can't control other people's happiness or unhappiness, but figuring out your own can have a butterfly effect on other people's lives also. So, yes, we are small and insignificant, but Willa, maybe we can change the world!"

I gave his hand a squeeze. "Thanks for that."

We spent the rest of the walk back into town talking about all the other people I'd come across.

When I told him about Steve, from the diner, he growled, "I hate that he said that to you. I'm sorry."

"It's okay. I was just glad that I had the honest excuse that I had someone."

He smiled, and my heart felt like it did a flip. "I'm glad of that too." He paused as if he was going to say more, but stopped himself.

The beginning of love is so sweet. To want and be wanted. I thought. My mind betrayed me for a moment as it ran to Peter. I wondered if he'd mind that I had found someone too. It kept running away from me, my earlier doubt creeping back in. *Was I only happy right now because I had found a new love? What if this didn't work out? Would I still be able to find my happiness inside of myself?*

"What are you thinking about?" Ethan's voice interrupted the cascading thoughts as they threatened to overwhelm me.

I looked up at him, blinking back sudden tears. "I just got really anxious all of a sudden. Wondering if I'm happy because of you, or because of the things I've been learning."

His expression was thoughtful, "Can't it be both? I don't think it needs to be mutually exclusive."

"I know," I agreed. "It's just I didn't want to base my happiness on a person, I wanted to find it inside of me."

"Do you think you're basing your happiness on me, or am I just adding to it?"

His question was so calm, so reassuring, I hugged his arm. "You're right. It's an addition. I got so scared there for a second."

"I think that we're so used to things going wrong in life that we're scared of being too happy. Our minds try to get us down to a manageable level so that if the bottom falls out we won't get too hurt."

"Yours too?" I asked.

He chuckled, "Mine too. You're amazing, Willa. I'm so glad that I met you. You have this spark of magic about you. I'd pretty much given up on ever finding someone that I could connect with as deeply and on as many levels as you and I have connected. It's so hard to believe that you ever felt like life was mundane, because you seem like you have such a fire inside you. It's contagious, and I love being around you."

I was blushing by the time he'd finished. "Really?"

"Really," he affirmed.

Ethan's phone chimed, and he released my hand so he could take his phone out of his pocket. We'd just reached the main street of the town, so we turned and I led the way towards the hotel.

"It's Chris. He's going to be here in 30 minutes."

"Oh! Okay. I hope the room is ready."

"Yeah, me too. I cannot wait to shower and put on some clean clothes."

I laughed, "I bet."

"Your room is ready." The man at the front desk declared. He held out the key towards me.

I had peaked my head in to inquire, but now went in to take the key.

"Enjoy your stay, and let us know if there's anything we can do for you during your visit," he said as I turned to go.

"I appreciate that."

Our room was just on the other side of the courtyard, and had a view of the creek.

"This is cute!" I exclaimed as we walked into the room. The decorations were simple, but made the room very cheerful.

"Yeah. It's great. It was a good choice," Ethan agreed, smiling down at me. "If you don't mind, I'm just going to jump in the shower right now. Unless, you would like some help getting things from the car?" He had lowered his pack to the floor.

"No, no, of course. Just get in the shower. I don't have much to bring in, except the little cooler and my bag."

"Okay," He grinned mischievously at me, "I'd ask you to join me, but with Chris fixing to be here…" he let the sentence trail off.

"Yeah," I agreed, my face on fire. "No, you go ahead. Enjoy!"

I went back outside to the car as Ethan rummaged through his pack to find clean clothes. By the time I was back in the room, he was humming to himself in the shower. These little things that I was finding out about him felt precious. *So adorable.* I smiled to myself.

"I'm going to go sit out by the fire pit while you finish up." I said cracking open the bathroom door.

"Okay. Sounds good. Or… you could stand there and talk to me if you want."

I giggled. "Won't that be distracting?"

"Yes. But in the best possible way." I could tell he was smiling too. "I'm almost done anyway, I'll be right out."

"Okay," I hesitated, I didn't know what to say. My mind suddenly went blank. How could I feel like I had a million things to talk to him about, and yet not a single word was coming out? I'd been looking forward to talking to him for days now and, now that he was on the other side of the shower curtain, I couldn't string together two words.

"Are you still there?" he asked.

"Yes. I'm having a brain fart," I admitted.

Ethan let out a laugh and peaked out from behind the curtain. "Is it embarrassing to talk in the bathroom?"

"Maybe? I just all of a sudden got really shy and didn't know what to say."

"It's okay," he reassured me. "I'm done now anyway. Want to hand me a towel?" He turned off the water. I came into the bathroom and pulled a towel down from the shelf.

He reached out from behind the curtain and I handed him the towel. Stepping back to the door frame, I waited for him to dry off. There was a little bit of rustling and then he pulled back the curtain and stepped out. He'd wrapped the towel around his waist and was smiling at me.

"You're so cute," he said.

"Thanks," I replied, but I didn't really want to be thought of as cute at that moment, so I stepped forward, lifting my face up to his for a kiss. "You just make me speechless sometimes," I murmured.

Ethan pulled me in even closer and kissed me deeply.

"Alright, we're going to get into dangerous ground if I kiss you any lon-ger," he said, releasing me abruptly.

I laughed. "Yes, yes we are."

Turning away, I looked back, the laughter still in my eyes. "I'll be outside waiting for you."

"Okay."

CHAPTER 21

I sat down in one of the chairs by the firepit. My mind was racing, and I fought to quiet it. Ethan was so smart, so sexy, and so kind. Weirdly old fashioned in some ways, but I realized that I found it charming. He didn't seem like he was shy about anything. I wasn't used to this. There was such a sense of security that I felt with the level of communication we had. It was like he didn't want to just know about me, he wanted to know me. But, not only that, he also wanted to share who he was with me. It didn't seem like he held anything back. *He's just amazing. It doesn't feel real. Why couldn't I think of anything to say when he asked me to talk to him in the bathroom?*

He stepped out of the room, and I smiled at him. I couldn't help it.

"This is nice," he said, motioning to the setup as he sat down in one of the chairs next to me.

"Yeah, it is, right?" I agreed. "And I like that you can hear the creek down in the culvert too."

Tires crunched on gravel and we both turned to look. A white Subaru had just turned into the hotel parking area.

"It's Chris!" Ethan exclaimed, standing up and walking towards the car that was parking in the spot next to mine.

"Ethan!" Chris stepped from the car, "Bro, sorry I couldn't meet up with you when you were at Fontana." The guys embraced.

I don't know what I expected Chris to look like, but I had not expected the tattoos. He didn't have any on his face, but it looked like every other inch of him depicted some sort of inked art. His dark hair was long and tousled and his beard, with flecks of gray, reached down to his collar bone.

"No worries. I'm glad you were able to come up here to say hi. This is Willa." He turned to me smiling, holding out his hand. I took it and joined them.

"Hi Chris, I've heard so much about you," I said, happily. Ethan's manner of introducing me made me feel so treasured.

"Likewise. I'm glad to meet you. Ethan says you're pretty amazing."

"Well, he says the same about you." We all laughed, but I could feel my face heat up. Happy, embarrassed, and nervous, I was glad when Ethan turned back to Chris.

"Here, come sit. How's Elsie?"

"She's good, man. One of the kids we've been working with relapsed yesterday, so she stayed to be with her. But she sends her love and says to tell Willa she's sorry she couldn't make it."

We sat back down in the chairs around the fire pit.

"Give her my love too," Ethan replied. "I'm sorry about the kid. Is she okay?"

"Yeah, she will be, but she needed to be admitted, so it was important that Elsie be there for her."

Chris turned to me, "I'm sure Ethan told you, but my wife and I run a house for people in need, especially young people. We just help them get back on their feet. Some are recovering addicts, like the girl my wife is with today, and some just have had a rough go of it. Either way, we're blessed to be able to provide a safe space and help in any way we can."

"That's really awesome," I exclaimed.

"What about you? Ethan said you're up here on an adventure yourself."

I smiled at Ethan and then turned back to Chris, "Yeah, it's definitely an adventure. We're calling it a 'Happiness Quest.' Been finding out what happiness looks like for different people. My mom suggested that it might be easier to figure out what my version of 'happily ever after' looks like in the woods, so I took a vacation from my life in Orlando to come up here."

"Are you unhappy?" Chris' gaze was puzzled.

"No, not necessarily. Just had been feeling pretty bland about everything. It doesn't seem right to feel like I am just going through the motions. I wanted to feel like I could break out into song and dance at any moment, just because."

He nodded, serious. "I get that, for sure. Have you found what you're looking for?"

"I think so. I've gotten a lot of feedback from the people that I've met along this trip. Ethan and I had some good talks about it too," he had been silent this whole time, letting Chris and I talk, but he was smiling at me, so I smiled back. "And," I continued, "I'm excited to put the concepts I've heard about to the test."

Chris was nodding, "I bet that's been incredible."

"Yeah," I agreed, "It has been. On that note, though, do you mind if I ask your opinion? Where do you find your happiness?"

Chris looked at me for a long moment before answering, then said, "I don't want to come off as preachy, but my answer is Jesus. Happiness, or rather, Joy can only be found in Him."

I had not expected that answer. "I can appreciate the fundamentals of Christianity," I replied. "Love God, love people. Take care of orphans and widows. But I'm not sure that I fall in line with the traditional beliefs about God. I do believe, though, that there is something greater than us. That being said, I'd still like you to tell me more. I don't want to limit myself to only certain points of view."

He nodded, "Alright, so this is the way I see it. I see happiness as temporary, something that can change with the wind. You're happy when things go your way, but, when something bad happens, happiness goes away and other emotions like fear, anger, and sadness take its spot. Joy, however, is something deeper. I heard it put like this once: Joy stands for Jesus, Others, and Yourself. When you put things in that order, your life feels like it's on track. That there is that sense of happiness, or joy rather, that comes from deep within instead of being based on people or circumstances."

I understood what he was getting at, but at the same time… "what does it look like in your own life?" I asked. "How does 'putting Jesus first' work for you?"

"Good question. It starts with constant prayer. I think that is one of the most important things you can do, keep yourself speaking in reverence to God all throughout your day."

"Is that realistic, though?" I questioned, "I'm not trying to challenge you, but that's one of those things that doesn't sound very practical in real life."

Chris let out a laugh, "No it's okay. I get it. It doesn't sound practical at all. It's more like open communication, I guess. It's like when you're sitting on the couch with your significant other, you don't have to be speaking the whole time. You're enjoying each other's presence and can speak whenever you feel like it."

"I really like that imagery," Ethan interjected.

"If you want it in more secular terms, prayer can be a lot like meditation. So, what I'm talking about here can be construed as active mindfulness."

I nodded, "Okay, that makes sense. Is that all?" I paused, realizing how brusque and rude that probably came across. "I'm sorry, I didn't mean that badly, I'm just wondering if that is the extent of what putting Jesus first means for you." I felt like I was trying to dig myself out of a hole. I was not at all comfortable talking about religion, it's one of the topics you learn to avoid in the service industry. I had gone to church with my dad as a kid, but now none of my friends were in any way religious, so it had been awhile since I'd talked along this theme.

"It's okay," Chris replied, smiling kindly at me. "I understand. I've found that when I practice being in constant communication with God, I tend to naturally want to honor Him. Like, all good things that I do are because of Him. I feel like I'm empowered to do the good that I do because of my choice to put Him first." He sat silent for a minute, then continued, "It all really boils down to love. God is love, and any and all aspects of that throughout life is evidence of Him. So, sharing that in any way I can, to others and also to myself really is, to me, the most important and best way to put Jesus first."

"I like that," I replied sincerely. "There was a woman at Fontana Dam that I talked to, who stressed the importance of love, especially self-love."

"Yeah, I remember you telling me about her! I wish I could have met them," Ethan exclaimed.

"That's cool," Chris agreed. "I feel like there's starting to be a shift, and people are finally starting to realize the importance of mental health and the part that self-love plays in that."

Ethan nodded, "I see that also. It's really a good thing. I hope it means that this next generation will be healthier and happier."

"I hope so too. The kids that we take in are far more receptive to working with the mental health clinic we partner with than the older people. But we're finding that everyone blossoms when surrounded by love and support."

"Do you find that these people that you help actually don't have people that love and support them?" I asked.

"They really don't. Most have bad family lives, and any friends they have are either headed down a bad path also or have given up on them. It's heart-breaking," Chris responded, sighing. "So, we try to love them as hard as we can and not give up on them. There's been times where we've gotten to a place where we've had to send some of them to more specialized care. But, overall, if we remind them of the good that they are, they step into that. Too many people and even circumstances have reinforced that they are either bad, or just nothing."

"Chris and his wife really do amazing work with people," Ethan said to me, "I admire them so much."

"Thanks, bro."

I smiled at Chris, "Yeah, thanks for sharing. It really reinforces the importance of love, and caring about people."

"Of course. I hope you and Ethan can come visit soon and you can meet my wife."

"We will," Ethan replied. I smiled at him. I found I didn't mind that he was thinking that the future was ours.

CHAPTER 22

"I don't want you to leave," he said, kissing me again. We were standing by my car, not ready to part ways.

I reached up and put my arms around his neck, pulling him closer. I kissed him passionately. "I don't want to leave, either. I just have those damn clients that want me to do their hair." I let out a mock sigh. "People. I swear." I said grinning up at him.

"When am I going to see you again?" he asked.

"Whenever you want. I'll be in Florida missing you while you finish up your hike." My lips were against his as I finished speaking, kissing him again.

He groaned and stepped back. "Babe, you are so hard to say goodbye to."

"Good," I replied, smiling back at him. "I don't want you to get in the habit of it."

"Oh, I have no intention of making this a habit, except for this part." His hand went behind my neck, and he pulled me to him again for another kiss.

"I can live with that," I murmured.

Finally, though, we said our last goodbye, and I drove away.

I was blissfully happy. There's no way I could have known two weeks ago how much my life would change on this trip.

I couldn't wait to tell my mom how right she'd been to tell me to go to the woods.

I had chosen a route home that avoided major highways. It would take me longer, but I wasn't in a hurry to get back to the monotonous thrum of civilization. It was a beautiful morning, and I rolled down my window. I left the radio off this time because I wanted to think. Some people think better with background noise, but not me. My one-track mind would get too distracted and would soon be singing along instead of paying attention to my thoughts.

There have been so many inspiring stories, could I make my life one also?

There are so many things I want to try. Take a class trying out all of the arts and see if anything feels right. Take music lessons, read more, find more activities to do outside.

I want to be around people that inspire me on a regular basis. I want to have conversations like I'd had on this trip. I felt so energized and alive.

I was passing through a town and noticed there was a playground on the right, I realized that I wanted to stop. I laughed at myself. *Do the things that make you happy, don't just want to. Go for it!*

I parked. There was no one else at the playground. I jogged over to the swing set. I sat down and pushed off, higher and higher. My laughter seemed to be the only audible thing in the silence of the morning.

I slowed to a stop and just sat there, enjoying the morning. Life is so different and so much harder when you're back in the city and have the worry of responsibilities, jobs, and bills.

I went back to my car, grabbed the happiness notebook, and returned to my swing.

I reread what I had written so far, immersing myself in the memories the words invoked.

20. Speaking of God, Chris's response was a surprise. I'm glad there are real Christians out there who actually care about people. His theory of God being Love and that Love being the most important thing resonates with the things the Fontana hikers said also, minus the God part. Ethan's mom also had her theory on love. Is this a pattern?

I closed the notebook. I felt a sense of satisfaction in that there seemed to be a roadmap that I could follow. But I also was starting to feel really over-whelmed. *How in the hell am I going to figure out my own path? In a few short hours I'll be back in Orlando, and I'm going to have to change my life. Where do I start? How am I going to help people? What am I going to do to be active? Even more intimidating, how am I going to be creative? Fuck, this is going to be hard.*

My mind drifted to Ethan, he had reminded me more than once how important it was to live in the moment. *This moment, this moment I am sitting on the swings in this little playground. It's a beautiful morning.*

I pushed off again, stretching my feet high up to the sky. I remembered that when I was a kid I used to pretend that, if I got high enough, my feet would touch the clouds. I smiled.

I let myself slow to a stop and went back to the car. It was time to go home.

Sleeping in my own bed is probably the most magical thing I've ever experienced. I turned over. The bed at the Airbnb had been nice, and the nights at the hotel and campground hadn't been terrible. But my bed on the other hand… I pulled one of my pillows in for a cuddle. *Maybe in a few weeks Ethan will be here next to me.* I smiled. Grabbing my phone off the nightstand, I sent him a text. "Good morning. Just woke up and was thinking about you. Can't wait to have you waking up next to me again."

He immediately replied with a heart emoji. "You are the sweetest. I can't wait to have you back in my arms again either."

I smiled and sighed happily as I put down my phone and got up.

My phone vibrated again. I reached over to grab it expecting another message from Ethan. It was Pete. My heart clenched. It was a weird feeling. I hadn't thought about talking to him in days, when a month ago, I had thought he would be my person.

A wave of guilt washed over me, combined with a little bit of panic. I was going to have to tell him that I had met someone. But he met someone first. This is the way it's supposed to be. It was still a little shocking, though, that I hadn't even thought to tell him that I had made it home. I had been too busy thinking about everything that had happened to me on my trip and reliving all my time with Ethan.

"Hey you! Are you home yet?" the text read.

"Yep! Got home last night," I responded.

"Awesome. Gina said you'd be home soon. Dinner tonight? Can't wait to hear about your trip."

"That works for me. Gator's at 7?"

"Perfect. See you then."

I sat down on the edge of my bed. This was going to be awkward; I could tell already. *I'll also need to tell Ethan that I'm meeting Peter for dinner, right? Wow, I'm so out of practice with being in a relationship, I haven't even had to think about letting someone know where I was or who I was with in years. This is going to take some getting used to.*

"My other best friend, Peter, just texted. He wants to meet up tonight for dinner at 7 to hear about my trip. Can't wait for you to meet him, I think you'll be friends!" I sent Ethan after a minute of thinking about what to say.

"Sounds like fun! Looking forward to meeting him," he responded immediately.

Oh thank goodness, I didn't think he'd be the jealous or controlling type, but you never know.

I got ready for work, humming to myself, and then laughed when I realized it was Good Morning, another song from Singing in the Rain.

I'm so glad that Ethan knew that movie too, I'll never forget dancing with him in the rain. I sighed. *It had been such a perfect moment. Gina is going to love this story. She had hoped I'd meet a prince, and I really had.*

I got out my notebook and added to it:

21. I'm so excited to share the stories of everything I learned with my mom, Gina, and Peter. Maybe some of my clients too. Sharing stories feels like another way to create and maintain joy. Even just remembering all the stories that I heard on the trails and how they affected me. I feel like stories have a way of bringing people closer together, and I'm excited that I can share this adventure with them.

I closed the notebook and put it in my purse. *I think I'll carry this around with me. Never know when I'll find more to write about!*

Gina was waiting outside the salon for me, "Willa!" she squealed, as she ran over to embrace me as soon as I had gotten out of my car.

I laughed and hugged her back tightly. "Did you miss me?"

"You have no idea. Tell me everything!!!"

"There's so much. I don't even know where to begin."

"Start at the beginning, obviously," she paused, and then asked quietly, "Have you talked to Peter yet?"

"He texted me this morning, asking if we could have dinner. Why?"

"I saw him a few days ago and he asked me when you would be home. There are some things he wants to talk to you about."

I frowned, "Why do I feel like it's important and you know what it is?"

"Don't tease it out of me, Willa. It's stuff you need to hear from him," she protested.

"Okay…" I replied, but I didn't want to let it go and now I was a little worried. It was going to be such a long time until dinner and answers.

Walking into the salon, we started setting up our stations, and I began the story. "So, the house was even more amazing than the pictures…"

The stories took all day to tell. Gina almost died laughing when I showed her the video I had taken in the woods and had her hand over her heart when she heard about how I met Ethan and how we danced in the rain. When I was finally finished telling her all of the stories, she asked, "So, do you think that you've figured out what you needed to figure out? I mean, it sounds like you've found your happily ever after on so many levels."

"I'd like to say yes," I replied, "At least I have the building blocks that I was looking for. And, honestly, I think I would have said the same thing even taking Ethan out of the equation."

"I'm so glad. I'm so happy for you, Willa."

"Thanks, me too," I replied, hugging her as we parted ways.

I saw Peter's car when I pulled into the parking lot and parked next to him. He was just getting out of his car and smiled at me.

Damn, I had missed his face. It felt like I hadn't seen him in a hundred years instead of just a month. *That smile just gets me every time.*

He gave me a huge bear hug as soon as I reached him.

"I've missed you, Willa," he said simply.

"I missed you too." *It wasn't a lie. I had missed him especially at the beginning, but I was getting over him.*

We headed into the restaurant. This was the place we'd met a few years ago. It had been at one of the trivia nights and remained one of our favorite hangout spots. We took a booth in the back room so we could talk.

"I want to hear all about your trip," Peter said after we ordered. "But I want to tell you something first."

"Okay…" I didn't know what to expect, so I found myself bracing for whatever it was.

"I've done a lot of soul searching this past month, and I've realized that it is you that I want," he said.

"What? What are you saying right now, Peter?" my stomach felt topsy-turvy.

"I'm saying that I don't like not having you in my life. It feels wrong. And, while I thought I was falling in love with Vanessa, once you weren't around anymore, I realized that it was always you that I truly loved."

"Why now, Peter? Why are you just now figuring this out?" It was a rhetorical question, because I was feeling miserable. "Peter, I knew I loved you from the start. And anytime during the past year and a half I would have been completely all about you and I doing life together. But I thought you moved on! I met someone while I was gone. His name is Ethan, and he's a wonderful guy. Your timing is just horrible. I don't know what to do."

"Oh fuck." He was silent for a moment, and I could feel my eyes swimming with tears.

"I don't want to say this, but I'm going to," Peter continued, "I don't want to put you in a bad spot, and I don't want you to feel like how I can see you're feeling right now. This is my fault. If I had paid attention to my feelings for you before, we wouldn't be in this situation right now. I'm so sorry, Willa." He reached over and clasped my hand. "Tell me about your trip, and about Ethan, and everything. Try to forget that I said anything, it's going to be alright."

I gave his hand a squeeze. "Alright, so it all began outside a little mountain town in North Carolina." My heart hurt and my mind was in turmoil with this new development, but I focused on the story, the rest I would try to sort out later.

I told him everything, I had started to skip over the parts with Ethan, but then realized that I needed Peter to understand my feelings. I needed him to understand that Ethan wasn't just a vacation fling, it felt like so much more.

When we got up to leave more than two hours later, he opened his arms and I stepped in to accept his hug. "I hope he makes you very happy, dear."

"Thank you, Peter." My face was in his jacket, and I could feel the tears had finally given way and were making a damp spot. I stepped back. "I think I've realized during my trip that I make my own happiness, but he definitely adds to it. But you do too, you know."

"Yes, I know that. We'll always be friends."

"Of course we will. Ethan is going to be here in a few weeks, so you can meet him then. I think you both will be friends, too."

"I'm sure we will," he replied, smiling at me. "I think I might need a trip to the woods, too."

CHAPTER 23

I looked at the schedule at work the next morning. Gina had taken the day off. *Shit.* I wanted to talk to her about the Peter issue since she obviously knew about it. Part of me felt a little betrayed that she hadn't warned me, especially after hearing about Ethan. But I also knew that she probably had felt like she couldn't.

Work seemed to drag by.

Chloe, one of my regulars, felt like the only bright spot on the day. I had told her about my trip and then asked her where she found her happiness.

She thought about it for a minute while I used the blow dryer on her hair. When I had finished, she grinned at me in the mirror. "Honestly, when I am feeling down, I make myself some toast."

I looked at her for a long second to see if she was joking. She wasn't. "You're serious?"

"Yes. There's just something about the comfort of eating a nice piece of toast with butter on it," She giggled. "Some days it's one piece of toast, and others, I eat half a loaf!"

I couldn't hide my smile. "I guess I'd never really thought of toast as a comfort food."

"Try it. you won't regret it," Chloe replied, enthusiastically.

"I will," I laughed.

As I drove home that evening, I still had this nagging feeling of dissatisfaction. Everything felt busy and crowded. The red lights, the merging traffic, the reaction of the cars to the traffic around us.

"Why was it so important for you to get in front of that car, you're not actually going to get there any faster," I said to one of the weaving vehicles.

How did everything, even the air, feel stifling, and how had I never noticed it before?

I pulled into my parking space at home and sent Ethan a text. "I don't know how to describe it really, but I feel really weird being back here."

"What do you mean?" He sent back right away.

"I feel like I'm suffocating. Or like a prisoner returning to his cell, not that I would know, but this is how I imagine that would feel like."

It was a few minutes before he responded, and I had made my way up into my apartment. It was hot outside, but I turned off my air conditioner and opened all the windows. I needed the fresh air.

"That's pretty normal for anyone who has spent significant time in the wild," he responded. "It's the same for me whenever I go back to civilization too."

"Well, I'm glad it's not just me."

"Not at all," he texted back. "I'm convinced our more natural state is found outside the confines of society. We're not meant to live like we do."

"So, we're moving to the woods?" I responded with a wink and a heart emoji.

"Yes!" He put a couple of laughing faces and a heart. "I wonder if the thrill that is felt when you're in the woods stays if you actually live here."

"Oh gosh, I hadn't thought of that," I replied, thoughtfully. "But a friend of mine moved to the beach in her twenties and had people tell her that she would get used to it and not feel the magic after she'd lived there awhile. She's been there 20 years now and still gets up for the sunrise."

"I guess when you find a spot that speaks the language of your soul it's easier to see the magic."

"Yep! So," I continued, "a cabin in the woods?"

"For you and me? <3"

"Obviously," I responded with another heart.

"Already looking at our options." There were a few more hearts and kissy faces.

I giggled. "I miss you."

"Babe, you've been on my mind all day. I can't wait to see you again in a few weeks."

"Me either."

I put down my phone. I needed to figure out where and how to start getting involved, what classes I wanted to take. *Where was my happiness going to be found now that I was back to normal life? Damien's friend had done art classes, and everyone I met seemed like they volunteered doing something. But what could I do? I've never been good at art, why did I think that taking classes would change that at all?*

And, volunteering, how do you even find something that speaks the language of your heart and is going to be flexible with your schedule?

Overwhelmed, I called Gina.

"Hey," she answered. "What's up, Willa?"

"Nothing much. Just got home from work. I'm kinda flailing right now, because I'm not really sure how to move forward. Also, Peter. I guess he told you what he was going to tell me last night?"

"Yeah, he did. I'm sorry I didn't give you any hints," she replied, "I just knew it would be best if it came from him. What did you tell him?"

"What do you think I told him?" There was pain and frustration in my tone. "I told him that his timing was horrible, and I told him about Ethan."

"Are you good with that decision?" Gina asked, "I know we've all been waiting for him to figure this out, and now that he finally has…"

I groaned. "I think that I am. There's a little part of me that feels like I'm giving up something good. But, Gina, Peter has had all this time to make a move, and never did. And I didn't either. I think that says something in and of itself."

"That's true."

"I'm always going to think that Peter is wonderful, I mean, we're best friends. But this month of distance between us has been good, I think. I don't feel like I'm on the verge of being in love with him anymore."

"And Ethan?" Gina asked.

"He's really a dream come true. I can't even explain it," I said, smiling, "He is a Prince Charming for sure."

"It sounds like it," she agreed.

"I know it probably seems like things are moving way too fast." I was justifying myself, but I needed her to understand. "Honestly, though, everything has just felt so right from the first moment that he took my hand and danced with me. So, I know it has been fast, but it's also one of those things that when you know, you just know."

"I didn't say anything. I am so happy for you, Willa. I'm really looking forward to meeting him. But what were you saying at the start of this conversation, you said something about feeling like you're flailing? That wasn't about Peter and Ethan?"

"No, it wasn't," I replied, "It's like now I finally know how happy and how fulfilled I can be. But I'm back to this mundane existence. I don't know where to begin to make the changes necessary to have that feeling here." My mind flashed back to what Jim had predicted and a wave of guilt rushed over me.

"Well, have you talked to the life coach lady?"

"No, you're right. It's weird. She's the only person from here that I talked to while I was gone, but I haven't even texted her yet to tell her I'm home."

"You should probably do that then." Her tone was motherly.

We said our goodbyes, and I texted Christy.

"Hey, I finally made it home the other night. Can we meet up to talk soon?"

"Yes, I have an opening tomorrow evening, does that work?"

We set up plans to meet at the same coffee shop as the first time.

I looked back through my notebook. *How was I going to adjust back to normal, but include everything people used to find their happiness? Jim is not going to be right!*

Exercise was a common theme and that was something I could test out.

I googled "Gym nearby". The closest one was a kickboxing and martial arts gym. That could be fun.

They had an online sign up sheet, so I set myself up for the kickboxing class tomorrow morning.

What else? Volunteering.

I googled "Volunteer Opportunities near me," and found a site that matched people with opportunities given their schedules and interests. Perfect! I signed up for that also. I was matched with a few different options, but reading the descriptions none of them really spoke to me. But I signed up for one that fed homeless people. *I'm sure that will add some meaning to my life, right?* I thought. *Does this work if you force it? God, what am I doing? Is this really my path to a happy life?*

"Alright," I told my brain. "Refocus." Doing something art related or creative was another thing everyone seemed to mention. *I know I can't draw or paint. Maybe I should try a pottery class?* I searched. There were several in my area, but mixed in with the results was a sculpting class. That might be fun too! I picked the sculpting class for my first venture into the art world since middle school.

My phone rang, it was Ethan.

"Hey!" I answered, "Everything okay?"

"Yes, I'm just tucked in for the night and wanted to hear your voice before I go to sleep," he replied.

"It's so early!" I exclaimed, looking at the clock on the wall. It wasn't quite eight o'clock.

"I know, but it's dark. There's no point staying awake after dark when you're on the trail by yourself. It's more important to rest and be ready to keep going when the sun comes up."

"I guess that makes sense," I replied, "I'm glad you called. I'm missing you."

"I miss you too. I hope you know I think about you all the time."

I smiled. "Good." I was so glad that he didn't seem to have any trouble telling me how he felt. My past had been checkered with guys that had always left me guessing.

"Did you see anything cool on the trail today?" I asked, shifting the conversation. Part of me wanted to talk more about what he was thinking about me, but I also wanted to hear about his day too. He had a way of sharing that made me feel like I was there too, experiencing it along with him.

"Yes! There were so many awesome things today."

There were stories of the antics of wildlife along the trail, stories of scenery that he had had to pause at to breathe in the beauty.

"I love telling you the things I see," he said. "I feel like I notice more while I'm walking because I want to have things to tell you about."

"I'm glad you do because I love hearing about everything. Seriously, Ethan, it makes me feel like I'm not a thousand miles away from you and that, while our days are so very different, we're still together."

"I feel like that too. Tell me about your day."

"I was actually really overwhelmed all day. It was that suffocating feeling that I told you about earlier. And my friend, Pete, that I told you about?" I paused, I needed to tell him, but it was so hard. "He told me that he had feelings for me last night, but I told him about you."

"Oh. I can't say I blame him," Ethan replied after a moment's hesitation. "You're an amazing person."

"You don't have anything to worry about, you know," I said, trying to ease his mind. "There was a time that I thought he and I would get together. But, Ethan, I don't think that now. You've totally turned my head. You have done things, you've said things, you've inspired and encouraged me in ways that no one has ever done in the past. I'm not giving you up."

"Thank you. I hope so," he agreed. "You've changed my world too, Willa, I hope we always make each other's lives better."

I could tell we were both smiling into the phone.

"Do you want to talk more about your day?" he asked after a moment.

"Okay!" I told him about signing up for the classes and the happiness toast. It was almost an hour later before we got off the phone. My heart was full again and so happy.

157

CHAPTER 24

I was early for my appointment with Christy the next evening. I brought my notebook so that I could go over everything with her from start to finish. I just really felt desperate to figure this out. What was going to be my life now? I grabbed my coffee and sat down in the corner. An old man sitting nearby reading his newspaper glanced up at me and smiled. We were the only two customers in the building.

I opened my notebook and began to read, lost in the memories of the previous two weeks. I was interrupted from my reverie by the old man coming to sit next to me.

"I just have a feeling that you need to talk," he said, as I looked up at him questioningly.

I smiled, "Maybe I do." I could pretend I was back in the mountains and talking to strangers just because.

"What's on your heart, dear?"

I found myself telling him everything. I don't know why there wasn't even a hesitation on my part. He just had a kind face, and I couldn't help myself.

The old man waited until I was finished to speak. "That is quite the story. I'm sensing a theme in each of those happiness building blocks that you have."

"You see a theme?" I asked. "Sometimes it felt like I could see a theme, but since being back I've been really struggling to put them all together. I'm meeting my life coach here in just a couple minutes, in the hope that she would help with that."

He nodded. "If you think about the happiest moments in your life, they are moments where you are giving or receiving love. I'm not talking about romantic love necessarily, just love. I think if you asked a lot of people, they would say that their wedding day or the birth of their child are their happiest moments. Days that they are surrounded by love coming from within them and being directed toward them from others."

"Okay," my reply was hesitant as my mind went through all the different things people had said. "I have noticed love come up, but not everything was love."

"Are you sure?" I swear his eyes twinkled as he asked.

I opened my notebook. "Okay, what about gratitude? Love and gratitude aren't the same thing."

"True, but gratitude expresses love. So, you're giving love."

"Okay, I guess I can see that. What about art?"

He chuckled, "Yes. Absolutely. Art is love too. You're pouring yourself into whatever it is that you're creating. That is a form of giving love too. Sharing yourself, sharing emotion. It also can be a form of meditation, which is self-love."

"Quietness in nature?"

"Okay, this one is a way that you're receiving love. You're allowing the stillness to fill you up, you're appreciating the beauty of creation, you're slowing your mind to the moment. So, you're receiving love not only from nature, but also once again, from yourself."

I scanned through the rest of the notebook. *Embracing your inner child, he would say that is self-love. Dancing in the rain, obviously that's love. Helping others, also love. Talking to strangers, compliments, community, he isn't wrong. It is all giving and receiving love. Even being physically active, more self-love.*

I set down the notebook, letting it close. "You're right. Happiness in all its forms does seem to be expressing or receiving love. So, what about figuring out what my purpose is? That's been weighing on me a lot, too."

He smiled at me, his eyes crinkling up. "Your purpose is to discover how you can best love yourself, love other people and love the earth. I'm sure you've heard before that God is Love, that you were made in His image?"

"Yes, I think so," I replied, hesitatingly. Chris had said something along those lines.

"You can believe whatever you want, but, if you can let yourself realize that your best self is the one that shows love in all that you are and all that you do, happiness will never be out of reach. Look for the ways to exemplify love in who you are, be Love. I promise your heart will be lighter, life will have more magic, and you won't get lost in a field of blasé. Step into your full potential of love, dear, and you'll change the world."

There were tears in my eyes, "Thank you, sir," I whispered, blinking fiercely.

"The only other thing I would add is that I hope that you fall in love with life itself. Do the things that make you feel alive."

My mind immediately went to dancing in the rain with Ethan and stopping at the park to swing simply because I wanted to. I nodded.

"When you embrace your life with joy, other people will join you. They will want to come fully alive too. It will keep spreading. Happiness is contagious, and you can bring joy to this world by embracing yours." He smiled, "I believe this is your friend walking in now."

I looked behind him towards the door, Christy was just walking in. *How had he known? Maybe he saw her in the parking lot.* He stood. Christy came towards us, and he held out his hand to her. "Your love for people is not unnoticed. You're making a difference, don't ever doubt that."

I saw her blink rapidly a few times. "Thank you! I needed to hear that."

She sat down across from me. I smiled at her briefly in greeting and glanced back in the direction of the old man, but he had disappeared out the door more quickly than I would have thought possible.

"Christy, that was the strangest, most incredible interaction I've ever had." My mind was whirling. "But I think he gave me my answers."

"Really? What are they?"

"That happiness is found in giving and receiving love. He said to be Love." I brushed away a tear that had escaped. "All of the things I learned in the woods ties back to it. But he said that my purpose will be found as I exemplify love in all that I am."

She reached across the table and gave my hand a squeeze. "He's not wrong. It's the simplest of terms, but it will change you profoundly if you step into it."

I gave her a small smile. "I want to try."

EPILOGUE

I don't think this Quest has an end. It hasn't been easy, but I have changed. My closest friends, Gina, Tommy, Peter, have all noticed a difference in me, and I've started noticing a difference in them also. I didn't tell them what I was going to try, I wanted to see if I could first. I mean, how does one act out Love in all that they are? Christy and I worked together to figure out my love languages, so that I knew the ways that I received and gave love the best.

I started volunteering with a group that helped the poverty stricken. Instead of serving food, I ended up giving haircuts to those who wanted them. It helped them feel better about themselves, and I felt like I was making a difference. I never did get into any of the artistic avenues. Between Ethan, Gina and Christy, I have let them convince me that I am creating art with hair styling. I have kept up with the kickboxing class that I initially signed up for, though. It's been way more fun and challenging than just going to the regular gym on my own.

I have made it a habit to take the time to run away to the woods for a weekend once a month to quiet my brain and recharge my soul. Ethan joins me usually, and that has been wonderful. He says that he wants to marry me, and when he asks, I'm going to say yes. He's my biggest cheerleader, encouraging me to step further and further into becoming my best self. Doing the same for him has been such an incredible experience. I have witnessed what the power of love can do.

We're buying a home in the mountains, so life is going to change soon, but we'll be together. Sometimes, when it gets stormy, he starts humming our song, and we go out and dance in the rain.

If you're wondering if I've stayed in contact with the people that I met, the answer is yes. I sent my happiness journal to Rita, and she has shared it with Emily and Damien.

Daisy texts me every once in a while. She's been working with a therapist and has completely changed the focus of her life. She said that she wants to read my journal next.

What did Jim say when I told him that the answer to my quest was to love, love life, love people and the earth? Nothing at all. He just said okay. No snarky retort at all. He is so passionate about truth and justice, I really admire that about him. He might get pissy, but I think it's because he cares and gets frustrated that other people don't.

I'll leave you with this, a life lived focusing on giving and receiving love has been amazing. I don't know if I'll change the world, but it's changed my world. Things around me can be horrible, but I can only control how I react. I still get it wrong sometimes, but I love being ALIVE!

THE HAPPINESS QUEST JOURNAL

Lessons Learned

1. It is what you make of it, "it is what it is" is a cop out. Building something with what you've been given, and with the people you have in your life, will give you a sense of purpose and fulfillment. Waiting for something to happen without moving in a direction is a recipe for unhappiness.

2. Quiet mornings listening and watching nature (and drinking delicious coffee) have some sort of magic too. I have a feeling I'll discover more in this vein.

3. Gratitude and Awe are instrumental in finding happiness within you, according to my old ladies at the café - the awe that I feel here, and the thankfulness that I was able to get this house, even if it's just for a few days - makes me inclined to think that they know what they're talking about.

4. Missing your favorite person can have adverse effects... and thinking about it feels like coming down from this joy high that I've been riding all morning. What do I do now?

5. Embracing your inner child

The silliness of making myself a flower crown, dressing up, and pretending to be a Disney princess, is so ridiculous. The adult in me scoffs and thinks the whole thing is stupid. But there is another part of me that just revels in it. That part thinks it was the most fun I've had in years. Maybe I should silence the fun sucking adult, and do the fun things more often.

6. Expectations. I guess if I'm honest, I think almost every time I've been unhappy it's been because I had expectations that were unfulfilled. I wanted something and because I didn't get it, my happiness was gone. How do I manage my expectations to prevent that from happening? I don't want to be ambivalent about things. Hopefully I can get further clarification on this during this adventure.

7. Don't be scared of strangers. They all have stories, and chances are, the stories will make your life better.

8. Family is important, but even more than blood family, taking people into your home and making them feel like family increases happiness on all sides. Genuine love makes such a difference.

9. Walking beside this creek is a revelation in the sense of the harmony in movement. It made me realize that the movement of the water and the movement of my body gives me the sense that time had slowed to the rhythm of my steps. It feels like for once I am not being left behind, but moving along with it. I'm not rushing to catch up or slowing down. I'm simply existing at the same time and flow as the world around me. I've never considered anything like this before, it's such a weird feeling. I wonder if the artificial rhythms of city life are a contributing factor to feeling off and discontent. Because this, this just makes me feel in line with the universe. I guess this is what my mom and Christy were talking about. It makes me wonder why anyone lives in the city. This is so much better.

10. I met someone today who reminded me of a bit of happiness from my regular life. The look on people's faces when I finish their hair and they know they look even better than before.

11. On that same line of thinking, being reminded (either by yourself or by someone else) of things that you do well is important also.

12. Dance in the rain. ;-) <3

At this moment I am so happy. I am grateful for so many things, for my mom suggesting this trip, for everyone I've met up here so far, for the beautiful weather, and most of all, the absolutely magical moments. And Ethan.

13. Being physically active and doing something in the service of others seems to be a common denominator for happiness in addition to being grateful and creating (in some form).

14. Loving yourself - Bethany said that it was critical to happiness and relied hugely on integrity. I don't think I've ever thought about integrity before, not using that word anyway. I've certainly known people that have not been true to their word. People that can say one thing one moment, but then act in the complete opposite. After these conversations, I can see that they really didn't like themselves. I bet that the guilt and shame of not being true to yourself or your word would build up eventually until you felt that all the time. Since I'm going with the Disney vibe, all the heroes and heroines in those stories are definitely noble, honorable, and kind. Full of integrity.

15. Contentedness – Mark's version of happiness was based on being content with what he had. He said that he didn't feel like he needed to have the next best thing, or achieve the traditional definitions of success. He had realized that he could be happy even with very little. When his wife had left him, he had to realize that he was not a failure, and that the single life had a peace about it that hadn't been present in his life, especially at the end of his relationship. He had said that being content with a little made it so that he was able to put his employees and customers first, and was able to reward bonuses and discounts out of his profits. He said because of these fair business practices, he had developed a bunch of loyal employees and customers.

I wonder what I can do to cultivate this in my own life. I love that he has been able to step away from the capitalist point of view.

16. Community

Noelle mentioned community, and how the lack of it really was the main source of any unhappiness that she felt. I don't think I've ever considered community as a bit of happiness. But I can't imagine living somewhere where I didn't know people. Even though it's Orlando, I see people I know every day, even if it's just on a trip to the store or a walk in the park. There's people I went to school with, regulars at my salon, people that I knew from past jobs. There's other regulars from places that my friends and I frequent, there's just always someone to say hi to. I can't imagine feeling isolated like Noelle said that she did, always feeling like a stranger, and having to make new friends every year.

17. What a weird day this has been already. Sharing what I learned with Daisy felt really good. I hope it helps her. This interaction with Steve just now was crazy. I don't even know what to say about it right now.

18. Ethan and I talked about so much it's hard to know what to say. Some of the major points he brought up were that happiness is just an emotion, and it's okay and even important to feel other emotions also. I loved his metaphor about emotions being like waves, and how it's important to learn how to surf so that you aren't overwhelmed. He said that it's important to keep moving forward and to find the happy moments even in the midst of bad things.

He's so good at staying in the moment. I hope I learn to be better at that. I really can't wait to spend more time with him.

19. There has been so much lately, things I haven't taken the time to write down, positives and negatives.

Happiness does look different for everyone. Steve, the creeper from the bar, had proclaimed that Sex, Drugs, and Rock and Roll were his tenets to happiness. I wonder if those things actually did make him happy, or if they just numbed the other feelings?

Jim said there was no purpose to life, that happiness was bullshit, and the pursuit of it was a waste of time. I will prove him wrong. I mean, he said he didn't like people so he spent his time away from them. Yet, he was the one that joined me walking on the trail. And he also chooses to spend his time around things that he likes. I wish I had thought of that while we were talking, I wonder what he would have said to that.

He said that I was happy because I was outside my comfort zone. He probably wasn't wrong about that. People do seem to naturally gravitate towards their comfort zones, and while it might not be happy, at least it's comfortable. That was my situation back home for sure. Daisy's situation, too. Her marriage and relationship with her son, both were comfortable, but lacking. Maybe due to communication. I wonder when she and her husband fell out of love and how it happened. God, I hope that never happens to me.

The pattern really seems to stay the same no matter who I talk to, with the exception of Steve (and Jim of course). Happiness is found in helping people or positive input in the community. It is also important to be active and creative. And then, maybe most important of all, I need to cultivate a mind that focuses on gratitude and being content.

If I look at my life just the way that it is, my happiest moments are when I'm spending time with my mom or my friends. And also when my clients looked in the mirror when I was done with their hair and I saw the smile grow on their faces. But, other than that, I can't really think of times when my heart feels as full as it does now. There isn't a lot of unhappiness, there's just a whole lot of blah. Neither happy nor unhappy. What are some things that I can change, knowing what I know now?

20. Speaking of God, Chris's response was a surprise. I'm glad there are real Christians out there who actually care about people. His theory of God being Love and that Love being the most important thing resonates with the things the Fontana hikers said also, minus the God part. Ethan's mom also had her theory on love. Is this a pattern?

21. I'm so excited to share the stories of everything I learned with my mom, Gina, and Peter. Maybe some of my clients too. Sharing stories feels like another way to create and maintain joy. Even just remembering all the stories that I heard on the trails and how they affected me. I feel like stories have a way of bringing people closer together, and I'm excited that I can share this adventure with them.

22. Happiness toast? I laughed so hard when Chloe told me that's where she finds her happiness. I never really considered toast to be a comfort food before, but I guess it can be!

23. Love is the core of happiness. I guess I saw that sometimes during my trip, but somehow, I didn't quite grasp it. I'm trying to be super intentional about expressing love to people, complimenting strangers for things, encouraging friends whenever I can, and becoming a more active listener. Sometimes it's easy to figure out what other people's main love languages are, but it's also been a great topic of discussion too. It feels like all my relationships are better when I know how to love them in ways that speak to their soul. It also has opened the door for my friends to love me better too, because when we talk about it, usually mine come up in the conversation and I've seen them make an effort.

Maybe the most important thing about love that I've learned, is that I need to make sure that I'm speaking/acting on my own love languages to myself. Wow. It's been life altering to not depend on other people to fill me up. I now know the things that I can do to adjust when the monotony creeps in. But I've also been intentional about letting myself feel all the things even when they're negative. Focusing on my moments has made it so those negative times don't usually last very long at all. I'm so very glad that I made the trip to the woods. What amazing people came into my life and how much my life has changed for the better because of it all!

ACKNOWLEDGEMENTS

This has been a project a few years in the making. I had always thought that I would write a book one day, but I let life get in the way. My own mid thirties were a struggle and I realized that I needed to actually accomplish a goal. Loving people and helping them become their best self has been something I've been passionate about for a long time, so I thought that maybe I could step further into that and become a life coach. With the completion of becoming certified, the idea for the book also came to be. I started conversations with some of people in my life who have been influences in the conversations in this book. In no particular order: Heath Ziglar, Ricky Miller, John Geib, Caitlin Neilson, Christy Belekevich, John Justus, Tiffany Garlick, Baylin Trujillo, John Erber, Erin Grafton, my brother Nathanael Edlund and so many others.

A Servant's Heart Ministry with Chip Hanna as the director served as inspiration with the difference that they make in Orlando's community.

Meredith Andrichak, Donna Laiosa, Besty Crumb, Eve Cammon, and my sister Erikah Edlund, have been instrumental editors and support on so many levels.

Vanessa Malinowski, Maggie Lathrop, Jennifer Grim, Jean Chen, Josh Bell, and others have been an amazing support system and beta readers.

Special thanks to Justin McRoberts for letting me mention his book "It is What You Make of It".

Honorable mention to Matt Shay and Happy Mug Coffee for years of friendship and great tastes and smells.

Dane Dupuis is an amazing friend and photographer, he and his friend Ina Visich created the cover photo for this book.

My father, Roy Edlund, designed the rest of the cover, and helped me whenever I got stuck in many other places.

So many other people have contributed and have been encouraging in this journey of mine, not the least of these was Erik Noftz. I have been so blessed by the people in my life.

The parks in the City of Winter Park in Florida, The Baker's Table in New Smyrna Beach Florida, Barnie's Coffee and Tea in Winter Park Florida, and Westfir Lodge in Westfir Oregon have been instrumental in providing the best places for me to sit and write.

None of this would have been possible without them and others. From the bottom of my heart, THANK YOU!

ACKNOWLEDGEMENTS